Apples and Alibis

A Down South Café Mystery

Gayle Leeson

Grace Abraham Publishing

Bristol, Virginia

Gayle Leeson/Grace Abraham Publishing
13335 Holbrook Street, Suite 10
Bristol, Virginia 24202
www.gayleleeson.com

Publisher's Note: This is a work of fiction. Names, characters, places, and incidents are a product of the author's imagination. Locales and public names are sometimes used for atmospheric purposes. Any resemblance to actual people, living or dead, or to businesses, companies, events, institutions, or locales is completely coincidental.

Cover design by Bridgeforth Design Studio.

Book Layout ©2017 BookDesignTemplates.com

Ordering Information:
Quantity sales. Special discounts are available on quantity purchases by corporations, associations, and others. For details, contact the "Special Sales Department" at the address above.

Apples and Alibis/ Gayle Leeson. -- 1st ed.
ISBN 978-0-9967647-7-3

Dedicated to Tim, Lianna, and Nicholas

Chapter One

Dilly Boyd stuck her head inside the door of the Down South Café and called, "Big Harry Ostermann needs a bandage! He got a splinter from his apple crate!"

At least, I *thought* it was Dilly. All I could see was her blue floral sunbonnet. But I was pretty sure it was her.

"I'll get it." I was ready for a break from the kitchen. Hosting a farmers' market during the fall Saturdays had been Dilly's idea—an idea that I'd thought was wonderful—but I hadn't realized how much extra work the market would mean to me and my staff. Today, in addition to Jackie, Shelly, and Luis, our part-time waitress Donna was on hand and Luis' younger brother Oscar was helping out at the cash register. Our "uniforms" consisted of jeans and blue t-shirts with the *Down South Café* logo in yellow. Since we sold the t-shirts at the café, having Oscar "suit up" hadn't been a problem.

I could only hope that all the extra work would mean a big boost in revenue. So far, the extra work had, in large part, consisted of pouring coffee and doing things like finding bandages and making change.

I stepped outside, squinted in the mid-September sun, and looked for the Ostermanns' booth among the crowded area. I'd roped off a third of the parking lot on the side of the building that housed our screened-in patio. Vendors with canopy tents or pickup-truck tailgates formed a semi-circle in which shoppers stood shoulder to shoulder as they sought the best produce, honey, eggs, and handcrafts Winter Garden had to offer. Winter Garden was mostly farmland, and the Down South Café was surrounded by pastures and fields of goldenrod.

The Ostermanns had a canopy tent and were using the back of their pickup truck as well since they had bushels of Golden Delicious and Red Delicious apples for sale in addition to pumpkins, tomatoes, peppers, squash, green beans, cucumbers, and cabbage.

I gasped when I approached the tent and saw that Harry was removing the splinter with his pocketknife. I was afraid he might need more than the small bandage I'd brought by the time he was through.

The big man chuckled. "Now don't be squeamish, Amy. This works as well as a pair of tweezers."

My eyes flew to Harry's wife, Nadine. She just smiled and shook her head. I handed her the bandage.

"Um...if you guys need anything else, please let me know." I looked back at Harry. "Unless you need an ambulance. For that, you'll need to call 9-1-1."

"I don't believe it'll come to that. I'll be inside in a little bit for some breakfast."

"All right." I hurried back into the café to find Jackie filling to-go cups with coffee for a couple of shoppers.

She handed them the cups and directed them to Oscar, who was ringing up another customer. As I stepped behind the counter, Jackie took my arm.

"Did you go by and say hello to Ryan's mom?" she asked.

"There were several people standing in front of her tables. I thought it best to come on back inside."

Jackie—my cousin-slash-best friend—just nodded. She knew me well enough to know that I was avoiding Ryan's mother.

Ryan. Should I call him my boyfriend? I'd been on several dates with the handsome deputy in the past few months, but I didn't know if I should be so brazen as to refer to him as my boyfriend just yet.

I hurried back into the kitchen to work on the three orders that had come in while I'd taken the bandage outside. I washed my hands, slipped on plastic gloves, and broke several eggs into a large bowl.

Half an hour later, Jackie joined me in the kitchen and handed me an order.

"Harry Ostermann wants a stack of buttermilk pancakes with a side of bacon, and Homer is here for his sausage biscuit."

"It's ten-thirty already?" I glanced at the clock. It was 10:27. Homer Pickens was a regular customer who came in every day at ten-thirty for a sausage biscuit.

When I had both orders ready, I took them out myself rather than waiting for Jackie to pick them up. I took Harry's order to his table first.

"I wanted to make sure you still have both hands," I joked.

He held them up. "I do. And I plan on eating with both of them."

"Is Nadine manning the booth while you eat?"

He nodded. "She's not big on breakfast anyway. She'll be in for lunch."

"If there's anything else you need, just give Jackie a holler."

"Will do. By the way, you should come out and visit our corn maze tonight. It's opening night, and we're having a bonfire, s'mores, hot cocoa, cider, ghost stories, a hayride... I guarantee you'll have fun."

"It sounds fantastic. I'll do my best to get out there." And I *would* get out to the corn maze...just probably not tonight. I had a feeling I was going to be exhausted.

Harry seemed to read my mind. "Well, if you don't make it tonight, we'll be open every weekend—Fridays and Saturdays—through the first weekend of November."

I nodded and took Homer his sausage biscuit. "How are you today?"

"I'm doing well." He jerked his head to the left. "Impressed by all the vendors you have outside. I think I'll check everything out after I eat."

"You should. Who's your hero today?"

Homer Pickens, now in his late sixties, had grown up without a father and, as a result, chose a new hero every day. Homer came into the Down South Café every morning at around the same time and ordered a sausage biscuit and a cup of coffee. I thought maybe he had a photographic memory. Even though Homer grew up poor and dropped out of school in tenth grade to go to work, he chose a new hero each day and could spout a variety of quotes attributed to the individual. Today's hero was Victor Hugo.

"Hugo wrote, 'There is only one thing stronger than all the armies of the world, and that is an idea whose time has come.' I believe the idea of your hosting a farmers' market here in Winter Garden has certainly come."

I lowered my voice. "Between you and me, I'm glad I'm only doing this for five weeks. I didn't anticipate it being this much extra work."

"But look at the opportunities and fun you're bringing to the town."

Smiling, I patted his hand. "Thanks. I needed that encouragement."

"Amy—phone!" Jackie called.

I took the call in the kitchen where I could put on my headset and work while I talked. I figured it was my mom calling to see how everything was going. "Hello."

"Is this Amy Flowers?"

"It is." I didn't recognize the voice.

"My name is Gladys Pridemore. I live on the outskirts of Winter Garden on the Meadowview side. I don't cook as much as I used to, and I wondered if you would bring me a few things."

"I'm sorry, Ms. Pridemore. We don't deliver food to our patrons."

"But I'll pay you extra!"

"That's not the issue," I said, as gently as I could. "We simply don't have the resources.

We're hosting a farmers' market outside the café today, and it's taking all our staff—and then some—to handle our workload today."

"I don't need the food right away. It's for to-morrow. You could bring it to me after closing. And it's just this once. I promise!"

I sighed. I wished Ms. Pridemore had made her request to Jackie. My dear cousin would have had no problem telling the woman, "Sorry, but that's not how we do things." I, on the other hand, could hear the desperation in Ms. Pridemore's voice...and could imagine it being Aunt Bess who wanted the food...

"Don't you have someone who could come in and pick it up for you?" I asked.

"No," she wailed.

"Okay, okay," I said. "I'll do it...just this once! Give me your address and tell me what you'd like for me to bring."

"I'd like some potato salad, deviled eggs, and ham biscuits. It's for a casual party I'm having tomorrow."

After talking with Ms. Pridemore, I got to work on my next order—an omelet with ham and Swiss.

Jackie opened the door to the kitchen. "Everything all right?"

I shrugged. "I'll tell you about it later."

"Ryan's here."

"Could you finish up this omelet for me?"

"No problem." She tightened the band on the ponytail that held her copper hair up before coming on inside and taking over so I could go out and say hello.

"I'll be right back," I said.

"Take your time. I'll enjoy hiding for a minute or two."

I was sure she would.

My heart raced a little when I saw Ryan sitting there at the counter. He was so gorgeous with his dark brown hair and milk-chocolate-colored eyes. It was his day off, so rather than being in uniform, he was wearing a black t-shirt.

He smiled at me, and my stomach somersaulted. In a good way.

"Hi," I said.

"Hi, yourself. How's it going?"

"It's a madhouse around here today."

"Mom is thrilled with how many people have turned out. Have you been outside to talk with her?"

"No, the only vendor I've had time to talk with today has been Big Harry Ostermann, and that was because he had a splinter and needed a bandage. But I did look over at her table and saw that she had attracted a good crowd."

"I appreciate your allowing Mom to participate. She loves doing her crafts and sharing them with other people."

I remembered Ryan saying that his mom knitted, crocheted, and did some woodwork.

"I'd like to take you both to dinner tonight to celebrate," Ryan continued. "My dad is out of town, and it would give you and Mom a chance to get to know each other."

"That sounds great...it really does...but I promised to take an order out to the far end of town. It's a one-time thing for an elderly woman..."

"We can wait for you. That's no problem. I'll go tell Mom." He gave me a bright smile before sliding off the stool and heading for the door.

I looked over at Homer, who was sitting on the stool beside the one Ryan had vacated.

"Why don't you want to go?" Homer asked quietly.

"Was it that obvious?"

"Probably just to me."

"I'm afraid she won't like me," I said.

Homer answered with another Victor Hugo quote. "Be like the bird who, pausing in her flight awhile on boughs too slight, feels them give way beneath her, and yet sings, knowing she has wings."

"What does that mean?"

"It means everything will be all right." He winked.

"Do you think Ryan knows how nervous I am to be around his mother?"

"More than likely. And I imagine he's nervous around your mother."

With perfect timing, Ryan sauntered back into Down South Café with one arm around Aunt Bess and the other around my mom. "Look who I found!"

"Oh, yeah," I muttered to Homer. "He's an absolute wreck."

At the end of the day, I looked around at my weary staff. Anyone would've been able to tell we were bone tired. Even sixteen-year-old Oscar, who'd tackled his first day at work with gusto, was stifling a yawn.

"Everyone did a wonderful job today," I said. "May I count on all of you to be back next Saturday?"

"Yes, ma'am," Oscar said. "I had fun."

"I'm glad. Could I ask one more thing of you before you go?"

He nodded.

From the corner of my eye, I saw Luis try to hide a grin. He knew what was coming—it was our usual Saturday routine.

"Would you help me divvy up the desserts in the display case?" I asked. "New employees get to choose first."

Oscar's brown eyes danced as he hurried over to the display counter and chose chocolate chip cookies and brownies.

"Anything else?" I asked.

He glanced at Luis for approval. I could see that Luis was shaking his head, so I cleared my throat.

"Just this once," Luis said.

"May I please have two pieces of the caramel apple pie for my parents?"

"Sorry, you're going to have to take the whole half pie." I shrugged. "We don't do slices at the end of the day on Saturday. Whatever's left has to go."

"Thank you, Ms. Flowers."

"Please call me Amy."

The boys said their goodbyes and left, Luis with his arm around his brother's shoulders. I smiled at their retreating backs.

"They're sweet, aren't they?" Shelly asked.

"They sure are." I turned to her. "Shelly, won't you please take this banana pudding home with you?"

"Honey, if I did, I'd have it eaten by tomorrow morning, and I'd be sick as a dog. Besides, I've got my figure to watch. Grandma always did warn me about the middle-age spread." She waved as she headed for the door.

"Donna?"

Donna was our part-time waitress. "I'd love to take a few slices of that chocolate cake to Bill and the kids."

I boxed up what was left of the chocolate cake and handed it to Donna. "Anything else?"

She shook her head. "This is more than enough. Thanks, Amy."

"Thanks for coming in today," I said.

"Glad to help."

I turned to Jackie. "It's just you and me. What are you taking?"

She blew out a breath. "We can't eat all that. The boys should've taken more. I think Oscar was too shy, and Luis was trying to set a good example."

"Well, I'm taking food out to Ms. Pridemore, so I'll include the banana pudding with her order free of charge. It'll be a bonus."

"What's up with that? Since when did we start a delivery service?"

"We didn't." I shook my head. "I wish she'd have talked with you, and then I wouldn't be driving out there."

"You're darn right you wouldn't. How'd she rope you into doing it?"

I lifted and dropped my shoulders.

"Let me guess," Jackie said. "Guilt trip?"

"Pretty much. I could just imagine it being Aunt Bess."

"Wait a minute...Pridemore..." Jackie raised her eyes to the ceiling as she wracked her brain. "Pridemore..." She brought her eyes down to meet mine and then hurried out to the parking lot.

"What is it?" I hurried behind her.

"I was checking to see if the Ostermanns were still here. If so, they could've taken the food to Ms. Pridemore. They live in a mobile home on her property."

"That's right. I'd forgotten about that. Their farm is actually *her* farm, isn't it?"

Jackie nodded. "I heard they have some kind of lease-to-own deal, or that they get the farm after Ms. Pridemore dies or something. But, yeah, they could've taken the food."

"Maybe she didn't know about the farmers' market...or didn't realize it was in our parking lot. Still, how weird is that? The first time she ever calls us for food—and *begs* me to deliver it—her tenants are here."

"Yeah, that sounds fishy to me. Want me to go with you?"

"No. I'm sure it's all right. She's probably just old and stubborn," I said.

"Still, you've never met this woman before. And what if she has a big mean dog or something?"

"I told her I would call when I got there. If nothing else, maybe she can come out to meet me."

"I still don't like it," Jackie said.

"Fine. You can come along."

After we dropped the rest of the desserts off at my house, I drove Jackie to the Pridemore house. Before we got to the property, we saw signs directing people to the corn maze. It reminded me to make this a quick visit so that Jackie and I didn't get blocked in or caught up in the traffic.

The large, white farmhouse was set about a hundred and fifty yards off the road. I couldn't see a mobile home or the corn maze from Ms. Pridemore's driveway, so I guessed the woman must have quite a bit of acreage.

I requested my Bluetooth device call Ms. Pridemore as we neared the house. There was no answer.

"Oh, well...I don't see any dogs around," I said. "Do you?"

"No. And surely we're close enough that they'd be running out barking by now."

"We'll just go to the front door then."

After getting no response from Ms. Pridemore at the front door, we decided to go around back. From the back of the house, we could see the corn maze, the apple orchard, the garden, the barn, the mobile home, and other small buildings on the Pridemore property.

I knocked on the back door. Again, no answer.

"Let's just go," Jackie said.

"But all this food..." I shook my head and tried the door. It was unlocked and opened easily. "Ms. Pridemore! It's Amy and Jackie from Down South Café!"

There was a strong, almost overpowering musty odor in the room. I pushed the door open farther and saw Ms. Pridemore slumped onto the kitchen table, an overturned coffee cup by her left hand.

I thrust the box toward Jackie and hurried into the room. "Ms. Pridemore!" I kept calling her name as I patted her arm and tried to rouse her. I noticed that her fingernails and lips had a bluish tinge. "Jackie, call 9-1-1."

"Already on it," Jackie said.

I looked around to try to figure out what had caused Ms. Pridemore to collapse. My head was starting to ache, and given the odor in the house, I thought maybe there was some sort of gas leak. I noticed that the stove was on. There was a Dutch oven on one burner, and it was on low. The pot must've contained only water, however, because it had evaporated. That or Ms. Pridemore hadn't put anything in the pot. I wondered if she suffered from dementia.

I turned the oven off and moved the pot to the kitchen sink. There were no other dishes in the sink, and the room was tidy. I didn't hear any hissing, and since the stove appeared to be electric instead of gas, I didn't think that was the problem.

"The paramedics are on their way," Jackie said.

"I sure hope they hurry."

Chapter Two

"The smell in here is making me sick," Jackie said.

"Me too." I propped the kitchen door open with a chair. "Can you open that window over the sink?"

Jackie scrambled over to the window, as eager as I was to get some fresh air into the room. "Huh."

"What's wrong?"

"Check this out."

Clear plastic film had been placed over the window.

"I guess Ms. Pridemore is already preparing for winter," I said. "Hopefully, the kitchen door will let enough air in to dispel whatever that is lingering in the air." I returned to Ms. Pridemore's side and continued trying to revive her. Her pulse was faint.

Jackie and I were relieved when the EMTs arrived. They immediately administered oxygen to Ms. Pridemore and loaded her into the ambulance. After a brief, whispered conversation, one of the paramedics decided to stay behind with Jackie and me while the other two transported Ms. Pridemore to the hospital. The paramedic who stayed behind phoned the sheriff's office.

"In cases like this where there could be a gas leak or something of that nature, we always report it to the sheriff," the young man told us. "Would the two of you mind remaining here until the sheriff or a deputy arrives?"

We told him we'd stay, and then all three of us stepped outside. I phoned Ryan and explained what had happened. I could hear Jackie speaking with Roger.

Sheriff Billings, a tall, lanky man with a solemn demeanor, arrived within ten minutes. He got out of the car and strode to the paramedic. "What did you find?"

"Elderly woman unconscious at her kitchen table. Lips and fingernails showed cyanosis. Weak pulse." He nodded toward Jackie and me. "These ladies opened the kitchen door to air out the room because they noticed a strong odor when they arrived."

The sheriff nodded. "Ms. Flowers, why were you here?"

"Ms. Pridemore called and asked me to bring her some food."

"I put the box in the refrigerator," Jackie added.

"Sheriff, I believe you know my cousin, Jackie Fonseca?"

"I do. Ms. Fonseca, I'll get your statement in a moment." He turned his attention back to me. "When did the Down South Café start a delivery service?"

"This was a one-time thing." I explained how Ms. Pridemore had called and requested the food for tomorrow. "Had I realized the Ostermanns—who were at the café for the farmers' market—were tenants on Ms. Pridemore's land, I'd have simply asked them to make the delivery for me."

"Nevertheless, you came to deliver food," said Sheriff Billings. "Walk me through what happened when you arrived."

I told him how Jackie and I had called Ms. Pridemore to let her know we were here and that when she didn't answer, we knocked on the door. "She didn't answer the front door, so we came around to the kitchen door. Of course, she didn't respond to our knocking on that door either...but we had all that food..." I watched his face carefully, but his expression didn't change. "So I opened the door and called to her."

"Was the door locked?"

"No, sir. I wouldn't have opened it if it had been."

"Amy was simply making every effort to reach this woman before we left," Jackie said. "And it was a good thing—had we not, Ms. Pridemore would be dead right now."

"Again, Ms. Fonseca, I'll take your statement momentarily." Sheriff Billings gave the paramedic a curt nod, and the young man came over to speak with Jackie. He tried to lead her away from us, but Jackie stood firmly in her spot.

Sheriff Billings took my arm and turned me toward the house. "All right. You opened the door. Then what?"

"The first thing I noticed—after seeing Ms. Pridemore there at the table, of course—was the odor. It gave me a headache almost immediately."

"And what did it smell like?" he asked.

"Musty...like the room had been shut up for ages."

"Continue."

I related how Jackie and I had gone inside and checked on Ms. Pridemore. "I couldn't rouse her, but I took her pulse and could tell she was still alive. While Jackie called for help, I looked around to see what might've caused Ms. Pridemore to collapse."

"Did you find anything?" he asked.

"Just an empty Dutch oven on a burner. I turned the stove off and placed the pot in the sink. Then I propped the kitchen door open to get some fresh air circulating. I asked Jackie to open the window, but there was a clear sheet of plastic over it, so she didn't disturb it."

Before Sheriff Billings could question me further, Harry Ostermann and his wife Nadine scrambled into the kitchen. Nadine's long brown hair was disheveled, and her eyes were as wide as saucers.

"Where's...Gladys?" Nadine asked as she caught her breath. "Harry Junior said he saw an ambulance leaving."

"And you are?" Sheriff Billings asked.

"I'm Nadine Ostermann. This is my husband Harry. We live here on the property."

"Ms. Flowers, would you please ask Ms. Fonseca to come inside, please? You may wait for her out there." He nodded toward the yard. "Ms.

Ostermann, I'll want to speak with you and your husband later, but Ms. Pridemore has been taken to the hospital."

"Wh-what happened?" Nadine asked. "Will she be all right?"

"We're not sure what happened, and I'm not aware of the severity of her condition."

I plodded over to Jackie and the paramedic. "Jackie, Sheriff Billings would like to talk with you." I gave the paramedic a half smile. "You get to babysit me now."

When Jackie went inside, I closed my eyes and ran my hand over my face.

"I'm sure this ordeal has been upsetting for you," the paramedic said softly.

"It has. I've never even met Ms. Pridemore. I came here for the first time today." I examined him a little closer and estimated him to be no more than twenty-three. "How long have you been doing this job?"

"Five years," he said.

"Do you think Ms. Pridemore will be all right?"

He lowered his eyes and shook his head.

After Sheriff Billings cleared us all to leave, he and the Ostermanns went to the hospital. The paramedic caught a ride with the sheriff. I dropped Jackie off at the café because that's where we'd left her car.

"See you tomorrow." She stepped out of the car but turned back almost immediately. "Wait. We never decided what to make tomorrow."

Every Sunday, Jackie and I prepared lunch for Mom and Aunt Bess. It was our traditional weekly gathering.

"Let's just make spaghetti and meatballs," I said. "And we'll take the key lime pie and the rest of the coconut pie we took to my house for dessert. It's not fancy, but it'll work."

"I'll stop on my way and get us a baguette from the grocery store."

"Thanks. I can make herbed butter." I smiled. "I'm sorry we walked into a disaster, but I'm glad you went with me."

"Me too. Have fun with Ryan and his mom."

"Yeah...well...wish me luck."

When I got home, I heard Rory's feet pounding the floor before I even got my key in the lock. I couldn't help but grin at the dog's unbridled enthusiasm, but I braced myself as I pushed open the door.

The little brown terrier jumped at me. I caught him in my arms and kissed the top of his scruffy head. He licked my chin.

I sat him back onto the floor and tossed my purse on the chair. "Did you have a good day?"

In answer, Rory ran through the room to the kitchen and back. I laughed.

Princess Eloise, a white Persian cat, strolled from the kitchen to the living room. Her head and tail were held imperiously high. She had been Mom's cat before Mom had gone to live with Aunt Bess. Unfortunately, Aunt Bess's allergies had prevented Mom from taking Princess Eloise with her. But the cat and I got along all right. Or, at least, the princess tolerated me and allowed me to do her bidding.

I fed both pets before sinking onto the sofa. I'd have loved nothing more than a nap, but I knew I needed to get ready to go to dinner with Ryan and his mother.

Before I could hoist myself off the couch to go shower and change, my phone rang. The number was unfamiliar.

"Hello," I answered hesitantly.

"Amy, hi, this is Ivy Donaldson. Sheriff Billings gave me your number."

"Hi, Ivy. What can I do for you?"

I knew Ivy was the crime scene investigator for the Winter Garden Sheriff's Department, and I'd seen her at the café a few times, but I had no idea why she'd be calling me.

"Gladys Pridemore is in a coma, and an electrolyte panel indicated a high level of carbon dioxide in her blood. Sheriff Billings told me you turned off the victim's stove and that you began to suffer a headache after you'd gone into the kitchen."

"That's right."

"Would you be able to go with me to the Pridemore house?" she asked.

I hesitated.

Before I could answer, Ivy continued. "I'm sorry. I know you had plans with Ryan, but the sheriff has already spoken with him and explained the gravity of this situation. I need to know exactly where everything was positioned when you walked into that room."

"All right."

"Thanks. I'll pick you up in twenty minutes."

After hanging up with Ivy, I called Ryan and told him I didn't know when I'd be able to get away.

"That's fine. I understand as well as anyone that when duty calls, you have to answer," he said. "Sheriff Billings said you had a headache earlier?"

"Yeah, it's easing. I think it was caused by the odor in that house."

"From what he told me, he thinks there was a gas leak. Be careful when you and Ivy go back in there."

"I might grab a light snack before I leave," I said.

"Go ahead and eat," Ryan told me. "Mom is hungry, and she doesn't like to be out very late, so we'll go on and have dinner...if that's okay."

"Sure. That's fine."

"I'll be happy to bring you something after you get back from Ms. Pridemore's place."

"No, thanks," I said. "I'll be all right."

After ending the call, I went into the kitchen and got a pack of peanut butter crackers. As I opened the package, I waffled between feeling relieved that I didn't have to go to dinner with Ryan's mother after all and feeling resentful that they were so amenable to going on without me.

I was washing down the crackers with a glass of iced tea when I heard Ivy's car roar into the driveway. I put the glass in the sink and walked out the door, making sure to lock it behind me.

Ivy drove a sporty blue convertible that necessitated her wearing her long, auburn hair in a French braid this evening.

"Thanks for agreeing to this," Ivy said, as I got into her car and buckled my seatbelt.

I hadn't realized I had a choice, but I didn't say so.

She backed out of the driveway.

"So...do you think it's a gas leak?" I asked, trying to make conversation.

"Too soon to say."

"I hope this investigation didn't spoil any plans you had for this Saturday evening." Attempt number two.

"The job comes first. That's a requirement of accepting it."

"Right. Of course." One more try, and then I'd give up. "This is a beautiful car."

Ivy smiled. "Thanks. My dad got me interested in cars when I was a little girl. I guess I always was more of a tomboy than a girly-girl. I could change the spark plugs in any vehicle by the time I was ten years old."

"That's impressive."

She nodded. "Dad thought so. He also taught me to change the oil, service a transmission, and replace tires."

"Wow." It was nice to learn more about the enigmatic Ivy.

"He isn't able to do his own vehicle maintenance anymore, so I take care of his car and his truck." Her smile faded. "He hates not being able to do it himself...but he supervises, of course."

"I'm sure he's terribly proud of you."

"Can you remember whether or not the stove was electric or gas?" Ivy asked.

Sharing time was over. "I think it was electric."

"Did you notice a heater in the room?"

"No."

When we got to Ms. Pridemore's house, Ivy frowned. "What's with all these cars?"

"Ms. Pridemore's tenants, the Ostermanns, have a corn maze and some other festivities going on for the next few weekends."

"Good grief. Why would anyone want to get lost in a corn maze?" She got out of the car.

I followed her to the kitchen door, and she pushed it open. Then Ivy stretched out her arm so I couldn't cross the threshold.

Gayle Leeson

"What did you see from this point?" she asked.

"The first thing I saw was Ms. Pridemore slumped at the table."

"Exactly where was the victim sitting? Was she facing you or was her back to you?"

"She was facing the door," I said. "Why do you keep calling her a victim? Do you think someone hurt Ms. Pridemore on purpose?"

"I'm not thinking anything right now—I'm gathering evidence. That evidence is pointing to the fact that Gladys Pridemore was poisoned by toxic fumes. We need to find out what happened so that if and/or when she's able to return home, she'll be safe." She lowered her arm. "Let's go inside."

I gingerly stepped into the room, trying to stay behind Ivy so that I didn't disturb anything. What I could disturb I didn't know—her train of thought maybe? Her line of sight?

"Tell me what you did after you came into this room," Ivy said.

I went through my actions step-by-step, just as I had with Sheriff Billings. Afterward, Ivy asked me if everything was as I'd left it.

Walking slowly around the room, I let my eyes linger over the table, the stove, the sink, and the floor. "Ms. Pridemore had an overturned coffee cup

{40}

at her left hand. That has been removed, and the table has been cleaned. And someone has washed and put away the dishes."

Ivy muttered an expletive. "I wish the sheriff had made it clear that this house was to have been left undisturbed." She took out her phone and called Sheriff Billings. "Hi, it's me. I need for you to coordinate with another law enforcement agency in the region...yeah...a full forensics team to help me determine how Gladys Pridemore was poisoned." She blew out a breath. "Sorry to hear that."

After ending the call, Ivy told me that Gladys Pridemore had died at the hospital.

I was glad to be back home. I took a bath, put on a sleep shirt and a floral satin robe, and stretched out on the white fainting couch in the fancy room. My "fancy room" used to be Mom's bedroom. After she moved out, Roger—my childhood friend and Jackie's boyfriend—added floor-to-ceiling bookshelves to the room and helped me find a reasonably-priced rolltop desk. I also exchanged Mom's bed for the fainting couch and added a peacock blue chair, matching ottoman, and a reading lamp. *Voila*! A fancy room.

I was absentmindedly thumbing through a cookbook as Rory snored in his bed beside the couch. At the tap on the door, Rory was on full alert and barking.

I sat up and slid my feet into my slippers. I was guessing my visitor was Ryan, but I wasn't sure. I went to the door and looked through the peephole. Sheriff Billings was standing on my porch.

I opened the door. "Come on in, Sheriff. I'll run and change."

"I'm sorry to inconvenience you. I—"

"No trouble at all." I hurried to my bedroom and slipped on a pair of jeans and a sweatshirt. When I returned to the living room, Sheriff Billings had made friends with Rory.

"This one likes his tummy rubs," he said.

"He sure does." I sat on the sofa across from the chair in which Sheriff Billings sat. "What brings you by?"

"Mainly, I just wanted to check on you to see if you're feeling better. Whatever it was Gladys Pridemore breathed proved fatal for her. Of course, I imagine her advanced age and declining health played a factor in her death, but still, I needed to en-sure you were all right."

"As you can see, I'm fit as a fiddle."

He nodded, but his brows remained drawn to-gether. "May I...see your hands please?"

I held out my hands, palms down, so that he could see my fingernails. I wore a clear coat of polish, but had they been tinged blue, it would have been appar-ent.

Sheriff Billings gave me a tight smile. "Thanks."

I lowered my hands. "I appreciate your concern. Did you know Ms. Pridemore well?"

"Nope. I don't think I'd ever met her." He rubbed his hand across his chin. "What was your initial im-pression...you know, when you went into the kitch-en?"

"How do you mean?" I'd already told him every-thing I remembered.

"Did you think Ms. Pridemore had suffered a heart attack? Fainted? Been poisoned? What crossed your mind?"

"I didn't know what had happened. I mean, the coffee cup was overturned, and Ms. Pridemore was face down on the table. I suppose I thought she'd had a heart attack at first. But that smell was there." I closed my eyes. "It was oppressive...more like a presence than an odor, if that makes any sense."

"Did your headache begin to come on almost immediately?" he asked.

"Yes," I said, opening my eyes. "I knew I needed to get some fresh air circulating in that room. And, of course, I saw the pot on the stove." I shook my head. "I thought that was strange because when she called the café, Ms. Pridemore said she didn't cook as much as she used to and practically begged me to bring her the food she ordered. She said she needed it tomorrow."

"What's going on tomorrow?"

"She said she was having a party...a casual party." I frowned. "But I have to wonder if maybe she was suffering from dementia because there was nothing in that pot. I originally thought she'd put the pot on the burner and sat down at the table while she was waiting for some water to come to a boil. That would've explained it being empty—she collapsed, and the water evaporated."

"What changed your mind?" Sheriff Billings asked.

"The burner was on low. Had she been waiting for water to come to a boil, it would have been on high. That's why I'm thinking she might've been suffering from some mental issues." I shrugged. "Of course, I'm merely speculating. I have no idea what actually occurred."

"Thanks for your insights, Amy. I appreciate it. And I'm sorry you didn't get to have dinner with Ryan and his mother tonight."

"That's okay."

He squinted at me. "Was this to be your first time meeting Michelle?"

"Kinda. He introduced her to me when she signed on as a vendor for the farmers' market, but we only exchanged hellos. They didn't stay for lunch because Mrs. Hall had brought Ryan's favorite lunch, and they'd eaten already." I pressed my lips together. "But, uh, this was going to have been the first time I'd actually conversed with her."

"You didn't gas poor Gladys Pridemore to keep from having to have dinner with them, did you?"

My eyes widened. "No! I'd never—!"

He laughed. "Sorry. I couldn't resist."

"I'm afraid Ms. Hall won't like me."

"The mothers never like the girls their sons bring home. The dads like the girls. The moms like their daughters' suitors."

"Really?"

Sheriff Billings nodded. "Haven't you found that to be the case?"

I gave the matter some thought. "You know what? You're right. I've never had a problem winning over my boyfriends' dads—not that I've had that many boyfriends—but the moms seldom liked me."

"Precisely. Works the opposite for us gents. It took my father-in-law ten years to warm up to me, but Molly's mother appeared to love me right from the start."

There was another knock at the door.

I asked Sheriff Billings to excuse me while I answered the door. This time, it was Ryan. He came inside without his usual kiss hello.

"Hi, Amy. Sir. Is everything all right?"

"Everything's fine. I dropped by to see if Amy had suffered any ill effects from...well, from whatever caused Ms. Pridemore's death."

Ryan's eyes flew from his boss to me. "Amy, are you okay?"

"I'm fine."

"She is," Sheriff Billings assured him. "And I was just leaving." He stood. "But before I go, Amy, what's Monday's special?"

"I don't know," I said. "I haven't given it any thought yet. Do you have a suggestion?"

"I could really go for some of that beef and cheese pasta bake if it wouldn't be too much trouble."

I smiled. "All right. I have my Monday special."

"Thanks. You two have a good night. Ryan, I'll see you tomorrow."

"Yes, sir."

"Jackie!" I exclaimed.

"What about her?" Ryan asked.

"I've got to call and make sure she's all right."

Chapter Three

I turned back to Ryan after making a quick call to Jackie. "She's fine. She couldn't really talk because she and Roger were walking into the cinema when her phone rang."

"But she's all right," he said. "That's the main thing."

"It is. I'll tell her about Ms. Pridemore's death tomorrow."

"I'm sorry you and Jackie walked into that situation." Ryan ran a hand gently down my jawline. "Do you want to talk about it?"

"Not really." I took his hand and led him over to the sofa. "I'd never met Gladys Pridemore before today. Unlike the other...deaths...I've encountered since opening the Down South Café, it was merely a strange coincidence that Ms. Pridemore collapsed on the one occasion that Jackie and I visited her house. Right?"

Ryan didn't answer. He merely put his arm around me and hugged me close to his side.

"I only wish we'd arrived soon enough to make a difference," I said. "And I'm sorry I missed dinner."

"Have you eaten?"

"No, but I'm not hungry." I'd felt a bit queasy since finding Ms. Pridemore, but I didn't tell Ryan that. Since the sheriff had been here inquiring about my health when Ryan had arrived, I didn't want to concern him.

"I'd be happy to go get you something or make you something." He grinned.

We both knew he wasn't terribly accomplished in the kitchen, but he could whip up something easy in a pinch.

"Did your mom do well at the farmers' market to-day?"

"She did. In fact, she sold so much that she insist-ed on paying for dinner." He chuckled. "Of course, she was disappointed that she didn't get to spend any time with you today, but she's looking forward to your having dinner with me, her, and Dad next Saturday."

"I'm looking forward to that too. I'm sorry I didn't get to visit the vendors today. Hopefully, I'll be able to do a little shopping next week. I seriously underestimated how much extra business the farmers' market would bring to the café."

"That's great," Ryan said. "It's just the butter on the bread."

On Sunday morning, I got up, fed the pets, and made myself some coffee and toast. I was glad it was still early enough that I could lounge in my sleep shirt and robe for a little while. I topped off my coffee and headed into the fancy room where I stretched out on the fainting couch and turned on my tablet.

After checking my mail and social media, I opened the Pinterest app to check out Aunt Bess's boards. Aunt Bess and her Pinterest boards were always interesting and often a surefire way to wake you up on a lazy morning. Her boards consisted of *People I've Outlived, Things I'd Love to Eat but Won't Fix, Lord Have Mercy*, and *Crime Scenes. Crime Scenes* was her newest board and my least favorite. It currently contained two blurry-but-not-out-of-focus-enough photographs: an interior shot of the Down South Café and an exterior shot of the Down South Café. The latter looked like just a parking lot—because that's what it was—but I knew where that parking lot was located. And, yes, my little business had seen its share of misfortune. In my defense, the first...um...misfortune...happened before I bought the place.

I didn't open Aunt Bess's *Crime Scenes* board. Instead, I went straight to my guilty pleasure, *Lord Have Mercy*. These photographs depict things—in Aunt Bess's opinion—in need of grace. A lot of grace.

One photograph was of a girl with "halo eyebrows" and a link to the weirdest brow trends of the year. Aunt Bess had captioned the photo, "Lord, have mercy. Look how much prettier these little girls would be if they left their eyebrows in the right place."

Another photo depicted a person with bread tied to his head. Aunt Bess's thoughts: "Lord, have mercy. What a waste of good bread. Does he know how many bologna sandwiches that would've made? Probably doesn't even care."

I was still smiling when I went to take my shower. Less than half an hour later, I was dressed in jeans and a baseball-style shirt, had on minimal makeup, and was walking to the big house carrying a bag of groceries.

Mom met me at the door and took the groceries from me. You'd have thought they weighed fifty pounds and that I'd had to walk ten miles. It was sweet though. I kissed her cheek.

"I had no idea Big Harry Ostermann was back in Winter Garden," Mom said.

"What?" Aunt Bess bustled into the kitchen and sat down at the table. "Tell me about this big hairy ostrich man! I'd pay fifty cents to see that...a dollar if he'd let me take a picture I could put on my Lord Have Mercy board."

"He's not—" Mom began as she placed the grocery bag on the counter, but Aunt Bess didn't let her finish. She was too wound up.

"When I was a little girl, some of Mother's people took me to the circus one time. I remember there was something called a freak show—you know, one of those sideshow attractions. I thought it was scary, and I cried—Mother's people had to take me home." She squinted up at the ceiling behind her silver-framed glasses. "Of course, now I imagine those were only people in costumes. But a hairy ostrich man? That really would be something to see."

Mom blew out a breath. "Harry. Oster. Mann. Not ostrich man. He's someone I went to high school with. He played football, and everyone called him Big Harry."

"Huh." I took tomatoes from the grocery bag. "I got the impression that the Ostermanns weren't from around here."

"The family moved away at the beginning of Harry's senior year," Mom said. "So that was nearly thirty years ago."

"Why don't I know these people?" Aunt Bess asked.

"Probably because the family hasn't lived here in thirty years." Mom made a face to clearly convey to me that Aunt Bess was getting on her last nerve this morning. As if there had been any doubt.

"No, that's not it." Aunt Bess shook her head. "I have a mind like a steel trap. I remember everything."

"But, Aunt Bess, you weren't living in Winter Garden thirty years ago," I reminded her.

She snapped her fingers. "That's right. I wasn't."

"The Ostermanns have been living on Gladys Pridemore's farm outside of town." I took down the cutting board and removed a knife from the block.

"Now, I know Gladys. I was never very fond of her. We went to school together, and she thought she was better than everybody else." She harrumphed. "Wore these fancy little dresses to school...patent leather shoes. I'd like to see her try to outshine me these days."

I washed the tomatoes and began dicing them.

"Was she there yesterday?" Aunt Bess asked. "At the farmers' market?"

"No," I said.

"Do you think she'll be there next Saturday? If you do, I'll get all duded up. Let her know she's not the only one—"

"Aunt Bess, Gladys Pridemore is dead."

"Oh..." Her face fell. I wasn't sure whether her regret stemmed from the fact that Ms. Pridemore had died or from the fact that Aunt Bess would now never have the chance to get duded up and show off to Ms. Pridemore at the farmers' market.

"Well, I hate that," Aunt Bess continued. "I hope she went peacefully. You know, she always looked so cute when she came to school... When her obituary comes out, I'll add her to my People I've Outlived board."

Mom's jaw dropped. "Aunt Bess!"

"What? It's an honor." She looked from Mom to me and nodded. "It's an honor."

"Of course, it is," I said.

"Who died?" Jackie asked as she came into the kitchen. "I heard Granny say she was adding someone to her People I've Outlived board."

"Gladys Pridemore," Mom answered.

Jackie took hold of the back of Aunt Bess's chair as if to steady herself. "Wh-what? I...I thought she was going to b-be all right."

I shook my head slightly.

"W-was there something else...something we could've done?" Jackie asked.

"No." I felt like going over and hugging her, but Jackie didn't usually appreciate displays of affection when she was feeling weak or vulnerable.

Aunt Bess patted Jackie's hand, and I was glad.

"That's why you called me last night to see if I was okay." Jackie stepped around the table to sink into one of the empty chairs. "Are you okay?"

"Yes, I'm fine."

"Somebody needs to tell us what's going on here," Mom said.

"And be quick about it." Aunt Bess was always ready with her two cents.

There was enough food left that I had plenty of spaghetti and meatballs to take to Ryan and anyone else who might be working at the police station today. Sheriff Billings was there, and he was delighted with the food. He directed me into the conference room that served as a lunchroom on occasion.

"Does Mrs. Billings have you on a diet or something?" I asked. I couldn't imagine why—the man was so skinny that when he turned sideways, he practically disappeared—but maybe he had high cholesterol or something.

"Nope. She's left me."

I stiffened as I wished the floor would open up and swallow me.

Sheriff Billings laughed at my obvious discomfort. "It's only for a couple of weeks. Her sister broke her arm and needed Molly's help until she gets used to the cast."

I slumped in relief. "Thank goodness. You had me going there for a minute."

"Well, you kinda had it coming—suggesting I needed to be on a diet." He took the pot from me and placed it on the table.

"I did not make any suggestions whatsoever. I thought maybe you had high cholesterol or...or something. I didn't want to get us both in trouble," I said. "But now that I know the situation, I heartily invite you to come by the café at closing time each day, and I'll make sure you have food for dinner as well as for lunch."

"I appreciate that more than you know. I never have been very handy in the kitchen." He nodded at something behind me. "Here comes your young man now."

"Hi." He gave me a warm smile but didn't touch me in front of his superior officer. I was appreciative of his consideration. "What smells so good?"

Sheriff Billings took the lid off the pot. "Spaghetti and meatballs."

"I have a loaf of bread in the car," I said. "I'll run back out and get it."

"Nonsense." Sheriff Billings held up his right hand. "Toss me your car keys."

I fished them out of my purse and handed them to him. I wasn't about to throw them and risk breaking something in a police station.

"Sir, before you go, I just got off the phone with the coroner. He's doing the autopsy on Gladys Pridemore tomorrow morning."

Once Sheriff Billings was out of the office, Ryan pulled me to him for a quick kiss. With a grin, he said, "Now I'd better get some plates before the sheriff comes back and starts eating out of the pot."

While Ryan was in the breakroom, I felt the sides of the slow cooker to make sure the food was still warm. It was, but I plugged the device in and turned it on low.

"Hello."

At the sound of the man's voice, I stepped out of the conference room. Ryan emerged from the breakroom with paper plates, cups, plastic cutlery, and napkins.

"Be right with you," Ryan told the man. He stepped into the conference room to put the stuff onto the table. He hurried back out and apologized to the pleasant-looking—I might've even thought *handsome* was he not old enough to be my father—man standing just inside the door. "How may I help you, sir?"

The man walked forward and handed Ryan what appeared to be a receipt or a citation. "I received this parking ticket and wondered if I could pay it here."

"No, sir, but you can pay the ticket online. Let me grab you an instruction sheet."

"Actually, that information—or at least the web address—is on the back of the ticket," the man said. "I simply thought I'd save myself some aggravation. Technology and I don't always get along."

"I'm back!" Sheriff Billings walked through the door with the loaf of bread hoisted in front of him like a scepter. Upon seeing the newest visitor—the one who had not brought the bread—he sheepishly lowered his prize.

I rushed over and took it from him, and he gave me a tight smile.

"Thank you, Amy." He stuck out his hand. "Sheriff Ted Billings. How may I help you?"

"I was just explaining to your deputy and your—" The man faltered. He obviously couldn't determine what function I served at the police station.

"Caterer," I supplied.

His eyebrows rose slightly at that, but I didn't feel inclined to elaborate. I was still ruminating on how nice looking he was and trying to figure out his status: Was he new in Winter Garden, or was he passing through? Was he single or married? Would he and Mom hit it off?

While all these thoughts were tumbling around in my head, the man was relating his parking ticket narrative to Sheriff Billings. I zoned back in around the time he said he'd moved to Winter Garden last week and would soon be taking over the town's medical practice as soon as he'd made some renovations to the clinic.

"I understand the town has been lacking medical care since Dr. Kent's departure earlier this year."

"It certainly has," Sheriff Billings said. "And why don't I dismiss that parking ticket for you? A ticket is a lousy way to welcome our new doctor to the neighborhood."

"I appreciate that."

"Would you like some dinner?" Sheriff Billings nodded in my direction. "Amy owns the Down South Café, and she sure knows her way around a kitchen."

"No, thank you. I need to run. But—Amy, is it?"

"Yes. Amy Flowers." I shook his hand.

"Well, Amy, my name is Clark Bennett, and I'm sure you'll be seeing me in your café soon."

"I'll look forward to it."

When Dr. Bennett left, Sheriff Billings put his thumbs in his belt loops and rocked back on his heels. "Uh-oh! Looks like you might have some competition, Hall!"

"No, he doesn't," I said. "But that man might be perfect for Mom...if we can keep him away from Aunt Bess long enough to get to know Mom."

Chapter Four

Dilly was the first guest through the door at the Down South Café on Monday morning. She'd taken time to put on some makeup and to secure one side of her cottony white hair with a silver barrette.

"Don't you look pretty this morning?" I asked.

She waved off my compliment with a flick of her wrist. "Nonsense. Could I get a cup of that French vanilla coffee this morning? I'm feeling like I want something fancy."

"How about Belgian waffles then? Some people might consider them fancy."

Dilly nodded. "That would be good. French vanilla coffee and Belgian waffles. They're both from the same general vicinity, right?"

Before I had time to process Dilly's logic, Walter Jackson entered the café. He wore khaki pants, a navy polo, and a navy tweed newsboy cap. He carried a long-stemmed pink rose.

"Good morning, lovely ladies!" He spotted Luis at a table in the corner refilling napkin holders. "And to you as well, young man." He handed the rose to Dilly before sitting down on the stool beside her. "How are you this morning, my dear?"

"I'm well. Amy has about talked me into Belgian waffles and French vanilla coffee. How does that sound to you?"

"I think it sounds fine." Walter looked at me. "I'll have the same please."

"And don't forget my biscuit," Dilly called as I turned away.

"I won't." I smiled at the thought of Dilly's daily visitor—a raccoon who waddled down out of the woods behind her house at dusk for a biscuit. Dilly never failed to have a treat ready for her little pal.

In the kitchen, I got a mixing bowl and measured out some flour.

Jackie sidled next to me. "Do you know how jealous Granny would be if she saw Walter and Dilly having breakfast together? She'd be so ticked that she didn't spot him first."

"True. But Aunt Bess and Walter could never have breakfast together." I sifted the flour, baking powder, salt, and sugar into the bowl. "I've never known her to get out of bed before nine."

She laughed. "Excellent point."

When the waffles were ready, I took them out to Dilly and Walter. I heard Dilly say the name *Gladys Pridemore.*

"I can't believe she died—just like that—at her kitchen table." Dilly looked up at me. "I'm sorry you and Jackie were the ones to find her. I know how upsetting that must've been."

"Did you know Gladys well, Dilly?"

"Fairly well. She and I were in the same Bible study class."

"Do you know whether or not Gladys suffered from dementia?"

Dilly shrugged. "No more than any of the rest of us, I reckon. She'd forget little goofy things sometimes, like she'd be looking in her purse for her sunglasses when she had them pushed on top of her head."

"I'm afraid we all do that," Walter said, with a chuckle. "I often forget that I've placed a pencil behind my ear, and when I go back to working my crossword puzzle, I look all over the chair for the thing before I remember what I've done with it."

"You'll see one of these days," Dilly said. "Enjoy your mind while you've still got it, Amy."

"Yep." Walter nodded. "*Youth is wasted on the young*. Now, who said that?"

"If Homer was here, he could tell us," Dilly said.

"He could," I agreed.

Jackie looked it up on her phone. "George Bernard Shaw said that. But neither of you have anything to complain about—you aren't wasting a minute."

Dilly grinned. "No, we aren't. When we leave here, we're going to the Biltmore. We're making a whole day of it."

"No wonder you're feeling fancy," I said. "I hope you'll have a wonderful time."

The Biltmore Estate in Asheville, North Carolina, was an excellent day trip. Mom, Aunt Bess, Jackie and I had enjoyed the jaunt several times. Maybe it was time for another trip soon...a girls' day.

I had a sudden thought. "Will you be back in time to deliver your biscuit?"

"Whenever I have to be out in the evening, I put it in a plastic baggie—open slightly—so he doesn't have any trouble removing the biscuit. I leave it on the banister. He always leaves the baggie."

Walter shook his head. "It's the darnedest thing I've ever seen. The first evening I was at Dilly's house when that raccoon arrived, he wasn't sure he liked me being there. But he's decided that if Dilly likes me, I must be okay."

Shelly burst through the door apologizing for being late. "I slammed on my brakes because I was afraid this cute little groundhog was going to cross the road in front of me. It didn't, though—thank goodness—but the precious thing stood up on its hind legs and looked so adorable, that I *had* to put my car in park and take its picture." She laughed and flipped a strand of her long dark hair over her shoulder. "I'll show you all the picture in a little bit. Anyway, then I just *had* to go explain myself to the sweet man in the car behind me. I mean, there I was holding up traffic."

Jackie rolled her eyes at me. She then retrieved Shelly's apron and held it out toward her.

"Thanks, Jackie." She tied the apron around her waist. "So, anyway, would you believe it? The man in the car behind me is Winter Garden's new doctor! I offered to buy him breakfast, and he said he'd be along in a few minutes."

I clenched my fists, told Dilly and Walter to let me know if they needed anything, and went back into the kitchen.

Jackie followed me. "You're really ticked that Shelly's late, aren't you?"

"No, it's not that. I met the new doctor at the police station yesterday. He's really nice and about Mom's—and Shelly's—age, and I'd hoped I could find a way to introduce him to Mom. But now Shelly has gone and swooped him up." I sighed. "I'm sorry. I shouldn't say things like that. Shelly is probably lonely too...but she has more opportunities to meet people. I just..." I blew out another breath and got to work on my next order.

"Be right back," Jackie said, moving toward the back door.

I didn't have time to wonder what my cousin was doing. I had breakfasts to prepare. More than one person had requested Belgian waffles after seeing Dilly's and Walter's plates.

Jackie came back into the kitchen, washed her hands, and asked if I needed any help.

"Not yet, but I'll let you know if that situation changes," I said.

"I'll keep an eye out. I figure when the doctor comes in, you'll want to deliver his order yourself."

"Maybe." I wasn't sure that I did want to if the man was already enamored with Shelly.

After Shelly delivered the doctor's order for eggs over easy, wheat toast with grape jelly, and hash browns, I decided I'd take the man's food out to him myself. After all, we'd already met. He'd been kind enough to patronize my café—whatever the reason— and I needed to express my appreciation.

When I strode out of the kitchen with the tray of food, Mom was standing just inside the door of the café.

"Mom? Is everything all right?"

"Everything's fine. Jackie called and said you were making me a special breakfast."

"Oh...oh! Of course!" I took the tray to Dr. Bennett's table and motioned for Mom to join me. "Good morning, Dr. Bennett."

"Amy, it's nice to see you again. I told you I'd be in to try your cooking soon."

"I'm happy you're here, and I hope you find everything to your liking." I turned to Mom. "Mom, this is Clark Bennett, Winter Garden's new doctor."

"I'm Jenna Flowers, and it's a pleasure to meet you." Mom quickly moved away and sat at an empty table.

"Ms. Flowers, would you like to join me? There's no sense in both of us eating alone," Dr. Bennett said. "Besides, I need someone to tell me all the ins and outs of living in Winter Garden." He stood and pulled out a chair for Mom.

"If you're sure—" Mom said, pushing back her chair.

"I'm positive."

On my way back to the kitchen, I passed both Jackie and Shelly. Jackie was taking coffee to Mom, and she gave me a grin and a wink. Shelly was taking another customer's order to the window, and she looked livid.

Mom and Dr. Bennett lingered over coffee for so long, that I expected Aunt Bess to call in a search and rescue team. Shelly still tried to pay for Dr. Bennett's breakfast—"because a promise is a promise"—but he wouldn't let her. He said he never intended to allow her to pay for his meal and that he hopes to see her again soon. That seemed to smooth her ruffled feathers a bit.

As Mom was leaving, I gave her an apple Danish for Aunt Bess. Mom gave me a pointed look that clearly indicated that I'd be explaining myself later. I didn't care. I'd seen her having some adult conversation with someone other than Aunt Bess, Jackie, or me for a change. Even if she and Dr. Bennett never went out, she'd enjoyed herself. I could tell.

Homer came in just before ten-thirty. "Good morning." He sat on his regular stool.

"Hi, Homer. Who's your hero today?"

"Today's hero is Howard Thurman. Have you heard of him?"

"I believe so. Wasn't he a civil rights leader?" I asked.

"He was that and so much more—author, philosopher, theologian, educator. He was a great man."

"Sounds like it." I poured him a cup of coffee.

"There seems to be some tension in the air here today, which is perfectly understandable. I heard about Gladys Pridemore and how you and Jackie discovered her."

"Did you know Ms. Pridemore?" I asked.

"Only in passing. She appeared to prefer to keep to herself."

Jackie brought out Homer's sausage biscuit and patted my shoulder.

I smiled. "Thank you, Jackie."

"Yes, thank you." After echoing my sentiments, Homer decided to share a Thurman quote with us. "I'd like you both to remember this today. 'Whatever may be the tensions and the stresses of a particular day, there is always lurking close at hand the trailing beauty of forgotten joy or unremembered peace.'"

Shelly brushed past Jackie with a coffee pot.

"And there's Shelly," Jackie said, "trailing close at hand."

Homer raised his coffee cup in a salute to Shelly. "And she's a beauty and a joy indeed."

She placed her free hand on her chest. "Why, Homer, you're the sweetest thing!"

And, just like that, Shelly's tensions—and mine too, for that matter—morphed into unremembered peace. Sadly, peace never seems to stick around long at the Down South Café.

When I got home, there was a note from my mother stuck to the front door. It said—or, rather, demanded—COME HERE. Not in any hurry to get to the big house, I strolled through the grass beside the driveway. It was a gorgeous day. The birds were chirping, the wind was rustling through the trees, tousling leaves that were only just beginning to show their autumn hues, and the grass was a vibrant green. I saw a patch of clover and stopped to see if I could find a lucky one. After all, a person going to visit her disgruntled mom could use all the help she could get.

I heard the screen door slam on the hill above me, and I looked up to see Mom standing on the front porch. I lifted a hand. She didn't wave back. Too bad I hadn't found that elusive four-leaf clover because my time was up.

I resumed walking and playing out the forthcoming conversation in my head. Or, at least, I *tried* to. I couldn't imagine why Mom would be upset with me for introducing her to Dr. Bennett. Mom was only forty-nine years old. She'd left her job as a sales associate for a popular retailer in Bristol to look after Aunt Bess full time. Of course, Aunt Bess didn't know that. She thought Mom merely took early retirement so she could "kick back and savor life."

Dad had left us when I was a toddler, and we hadn't seen him since. And although Mom had dated on and off since their divorce, her social life had been practically nonexistent for the past couple of years. I thought it was high time she started enjoying herself more.

That's what I'd planned on saying. I lifted my chin and quickened my stride. Stepping onto the porch, I opened my mouth to speak. Mom didn't give me the chance.

"What were you and Jackie thinking?" She folded her arms across her chest.

"Huh?" Yep. That was my well-thought-out, intelligent comeback—*huh.*

"You heard me."

I had no idea where those valid reasons I'd come up with on my way up the hill had disappeared to, but they were certainly not on the tip of my tongue. I looked down at the porch flooring to see if I'd dropped them. Nope. Not even the sliver of an idea for me to grasp onto.

"Well...you see...I met Dr. Bennett yesterday...at the police station, as a matter of fact. Funny story...he came in to pay a parking ticket. I meant to tell you and Aunt Bess about it earlier, but it was beginning to get late when I got back, and I thought—"

"Amy."

I shrugged. "I thought he'd be perfect for you." Sometimes a body has no choice whatsoever but to tell the simple, unvarnished truth.

"What made you think that?"

"Um...he seemed really nice. He's new in town..."

"Right." Her voice was flat. "He's a man, and he's in the proper age range. I'm guessing that's all it took."

I huffed. "There was more to it than that!"

"What then?"

"Shelly was trying to reel him in, and you hadn't even got the chance to meet him yet!"

Mom bobbed her head. "So, that's it. You and Jackie called and had me rush to the café to get in line ahead of Shelly at the new guy meet-and-greet."

"Well, actually, Shelly was already at the head of the line, so we...you know...kinda gave you the backstage pass." I locked onto her angry green gaze. "Why are you so upset about this?"

"Because you made me look desperate! Not only to Dr. Bennett but to Shelly and everyone else in that dining room. You threw me at that man, and I didn't appreciate it."

"I'm sorry."

"You should be. It put him and me into an awkward position." She brushed a stray hair off her forehead. "I'm sure he felt he had no choice but to invite me to sit down."

"I'm really sorry." I started to tell her that it wasn't even my idea and that I didn't realize what Jackie had done until Mom walked into the café, but I didn't want to toss my cousin under the bus. Besides, I carried my share of the blame—I didn't have to introduce Mom to the doctor. "I'll never do anything like that again."

"See that you don't," Mom said.

"And I'm sorry you and Dr. Bennett didn't hit it off."

"Says who?" She arched a brow. "We're going out on Wednesday. Keep the evening free and tell Jackie to do the same. You two are staying with Aunt Bess."

Chapter Five

I was in the kitchen trying to determine what I might offer for the special of the day tomorrow when Sarah called. Sarah had been one of my very best friends since elementary school. Since her boyfriend John attended law school in Grundy and was away all week, and since Ryan worked odd shifts, she and I often got together throughout the week for dinner and games of *Scrabble* or *Yahtzee*.

"Do you have plans for this evening?" Sarah asked.

"Hopefully, I do now." I laughed. "How would you like to try this recipe for stuffed bell pepper casserole I found?"

"That sounds great. I'll be right over."

When Sarah arrived, I had just drained the browned ground sirloin, onion, peppers, and garlic. She closed her eyes and sniffed the air.

"Smells fantastic. Is it done yet?" She dropped her purse onto a chair and adjusted her ivory, off-the-shoulder sweater.

"Not quite." I transferred the mixture from the colander back to the skillet. "Did you and John have a good weekend?"

"Saturday was nice, but he had to go back early Sunday and study." She watched me stir in the tomatoes and uncooked rice. "I won't ask about your weekend. I saw Jackie at the post office a little while ago, so I know about the two of you finding Gladys Pridemore."

"Yeah...that was rough." I added oregano, Worchester sauce, and basil. "I'm sorry we weren't able to get there in time to help her."

"Does the sheriff think Ms. Pridemore died of natural causes?"

"No. He thinks she was poisoned by a gas leak or something." I narrowed my eyes. "Why?"

She raised and dropped one well-toned, mahogany shoulder. "Just curious."

"I know you better than that. What are you thinking?"

"It's probably nothing, but Ms. Pridemore came into the office to talk with Billy a few days ago."

Sarah worked for Billy Hancock, Winter Garden's one and only resident attorney.

"And?" I prompted.

"Well, Billy wasn't even her attorney. She just wanted some legal advice about the rent-to-own agreement she'd entered into with Harry and Nadine Ostermann."

I added the cheese, transferred the mixture to a casserole dish, and placed the dish in the preheated oven. "Was she unhappy with the agreement?"

"She wanted to dissolve it."

"Can she do that?" I asked, setting the oven timer and motioning for Sarah to follow me into the living room.

"Under certain conditions." Sarah explained that a rent-to-own agreement is basically two agreements—a lease agreement and a purchase option. "The title remains with the landlord until the tenant exercises the option and buys the property. But in Ms. Pridemore's case, she didn't charge the Ostermanns an upfront fee for the purchase option. Instead, the Ostermanns were to take possession of the property upon her death."

She and I sat on the floor on opposite sides of the coffee table, and I opened the *Yahtzee* box. We were lucky that Rory was occupied outside at the moment because, otherwise, he'd be fighting us for the dice. I had to be really careful with small objects around that dog.

"You don't think the Ostermanns did Ms. Pridemore in so she wouldn't break the agreement, do you?" I chuckled when I said it, but Sarah didn't look amused.

"I don't know what to think."

I rolled one die to see who would go first. I got a four. "Aren't agreements like that designed to be almost impossible to break?"

"For the most part, yes." Sarah rolled a three and handed me her die. "But there are clauses, as in any agreement, that can invalidate the contract. And since Billy and I got the impression that Ms. Pridemore's attorney drew up the rent-to-own agreement, then there were probably more clauses skewed to her benefit."

"Okay." I rolled and decided to try for a straight since I had a one, a two, and a three. "I take it Ms. Pridemore found some sort of loophole?"

"Maybe. She came to Billy with the contract because her attorney is currently in the Caribbean, and Billy thought her argument was tenuous," Sarah said. "Ms. Pridemore had a clause stating that the Ostermanns were not permitted to open up the mobile home to boarders."

My next roll gave me two fours. "And did they? Move in boarders?"

"Not exactly." She sighed. "Harry Junior—HJ—and his wife had a falling out. I understand they're in the process of divorcing. HJ moved in with his parents."

I gaped at her. "She can negate the contract because Harry and Nadine allowed their son to move in with them?"

"Billy didn't think so. The legal definition of a *boarder* is one who is provided food and lodging *for a price*. It's doubtful that HJ is paying rent to his Mom and Dad. I believe the contract originally intended that the Ostermanns remain on the property in the mobile home and not lease it out to someone else prior to Ms. Pridemore's death."

"That sounds like one mixed up contract to me." I finished up with a five and was able to claim a large straight. I handed the cup to Sarah.

"It was. Of course, everything I'm telling you is in confidence—even though Ms. Pridemore wasn't Billy's client, I don't want him to think I'm spreading gossip—but I think the woman simply changed her mind and was looking for a way to break the contract."

"Did she have any heirs? I mean, I wouldn't have thought she'd have made the agreement with Harry and Nadine Ostermann if she had children to whom she could leave the property."

Sarah shook out the dice. "She didn't."

"Then why did she change her mind?"

"That's the million-dollar question."

Once we'd finished our game of *Yahtzee*—I won, yay!—Sarah and I sat on the sofa and drank chocolate-coconut flavored tea. Rory had tired himself out and had come inside to doze by my feet.

"This tea is really good," Sarah said. "I never even knew chocolate flavored tea was a thing. Leave it to you to make the most interesting discoveries."

"I'm glad *someone* appreciates my ideas today." I told her about meeting Dr. Bennett, thinking he'd be a great match for Mom, and then feeling frustrated when Shelly met him and had seemed to wrangle him onto her hook.

Sarah folded her legs beneath her and sipped her tea. "So, what did you do?"

"I told Jackie."

"Oh, my goodness!" Sarah laughed.

I explained how Jackie had called Mom and told her I was making her a special breakfast but had failed to warn me before Mom arrived at the café. "To make a long story short, Mom now has a date with Dr. Bennett, but Jackie and I have been volunteered to stay with Aunt Bess on Wednesday evening."

"And what is Aunt Bess thinking of all of this? Has she met the new doctor yet?"

"She hasn't met him, and your guess is as good as mine as to what she's thinking. I'm sure I'll find out on Wednesday."

"I wouldn't mind a front-row seat to that," Sarah said. "If you'd like me to join you, let me know."

"That'd be terrific. We could play cards." I figured Jackie and I would need all the help we could get to keep Aunt Bess's mind off the fact that Mom had a date and she didn't.

My thoughts abruptly shifted to Gladys Pridemore.

"Also, would you and John be interested in going to the corn maze on Friday night?" I asked.

"I'll ask him and get back to you. We talked about visiting one last year but never got around to it. Which one are you considering?"

"The one on Gladys Pridemore's property."

Sarah grinned. "Do you want to find your way through a corn maze or investigate a suspicious death?"

"Who says we can't do both?"

The first thing Jackie said to me when she came through the door on Tuesday morning was: "I got a call from Aunt Jenna."

"Consider yourself lucky—I got a summons and had to appear in person."

"So, I guess we're babysitting Granny on Wednesday."

"Looks that way. I told Sarah about it last night. She's up for joining us for a card game." I finished wiping down the counter.

Apples and Alibis

"A card game would be fun." She paused to consider. "We could have some good food...maybe convince Granny that Aunt Jenna is the one missing out."

I nodded. "That's what I was thinking."

"I don't know why Aunt Jenna got so ticked off at us. We were trying to do the woman a favor." She readied a pot of decaf coffee since I was working on the dark roast. "And, apparently, we *did* do her a favor since she accepted a date with the guy."

"She said we made her look desperate."

Jackie scoffed. "We did no such thing."

Since I could kinda see both sides, I changed the subject. "Do you and Roger have plans for Friday?"

"Nothing in stone." She finished up the decaf and moved on to making a pot of French vanilla. "Why?"

"I'd like to go to the corn maze on Friday night. I haven't spoken to Ryan about it yet, but Sarah said she and John might be free."

"The corn maze at the Pridemore farm?"

"Yeah," I said.

"I...um...I'll let you know."

It wasn't like my cousin to be squeamish, so I doubted her hesitation stemmed from our finding Ms. Pridemore on Saturday. I didn't have time to question her about it—I had too much kitchen prep

{ 85 }

left to do before our patrons began arriving. Besides, I could tell from her closed expression that I wouldn't get any answers right now anyway.

It was such a busy morning that I barely had any time to even step out of the kitchen. When I did, it was to hear Homer telling a dour-looking man wearing a black toupee, "'You can't help getting older, but you don't have to get old.'"

My eyes widened as I hurried over to Homer. "Is that a quote from today's hero?"

"It most certainly is." He favored me with a broad smile. "Today's hero is George Burns, nee Nathan Birnbaum. Did you know that man was successful in vaudeville, radio, television, and film? And he lived to be a hundred years old."

"That's remarkable." I smiled. "Mr. Burns was a funny man."

Homer nodded. "Before you came out of the kitchen, I was explaining to Mr. Pridemore here that Mr. Burns had a humorous take on aging. He once said, 'When I was a boy, the Dead Sea was only sick.'" He laughed.

I managed a chuckle before turning to the man seated at Homer's right. "Mr. Pridemore...you're related to Gladys?"

"By marriage. My name is Malcolm Pridemore. Gladys was my sister-in-law."

Though he'd introduced himself, he didn't offer to shake hands, so I didn't either. "I'm terribly sorry for your loss."

"Thank you."

"Did you just get into town today?" I asked.

"No. I've been in the area for the past month."

"Oh?"

He sniffed. "I've been subjected to the Golden Age of Comedy hour and been forced to engage in a game of twenty questions. Might I get some service now?"

"Of course," I said. I took Mr. Pridemore's precise order for eggs slightly over easy, bacon that was crispy but not burned, and orange juice that was freshly squeezed with no pulp.

"If my order is in any way incorrect, I absolutely will not pay," Mr. Pridemore said.

As I turned to go back to the kitchen, Homer cleared his throat. I froze and then risked a peek over my shoulder.

"Another thing Mr. Burns said was, 'I was brought up to respect my elders, so now I don't have to respect anybody.' I reckon you must adhere to that same philosophy, Mr. Pridemore."

I hurried on into the kitchen to start on the breakfast order for which Mr. Pridemore would likely refuse to pay.

A few minutes later, as I delivered Mr. Pridemore's meal, I noticed Homer paying his bill. Jackie, who was at the register, handed him a bakery bag. They exchanged some quiet words before Homer grinned and left.

Jackie joined me in the kitchen afterward and asked me if I needed any help.

"No, thanks. I'm fine," I said. "By the way, what was in Homer's takeout bag?"

"A blueberry muffin and two oatmeal raisin cookies." She gave me a mischievous grin. "I overheard his conversation with Malcolm Pridemore and felt like he deserved them."

"Agreed. Thanks for rewarding him."

She glanced through the window between the kitchen and the dining room. "Well, if that man who is eating his breakfast like someone who hasn't had a bite in days thinks we're going to comp him for a meal he has nearly finished, he's sadly mistaken."

"Today is the first time I've ever seen Mr. Pridemore, although he says he's been in this region for a month." I whisked together eggs and milk. "Do you think he recently moved to Winter Garden?"

"I think he's trying to," Jackie said. "Before he got tired of talking with Homer, I heard him say he'd hoped to buy his sister-in-law's property."

"Huh." Although I didn't mention it to Jackie, I wondered what would become of Gladys Pridemore's property now that she was dead. Had she had the opportunity to revoke the Ostermann's rent-to-own agreement? Or would the Ostermanns now inherit in accordance with the agreement and Ms. Pridemore's will? I also wondered if it had been Malcolm Pridemore who'd urged her to break the contract in an effort to get her to sell him the property.

Chapter Six

It wasn't until nearly two-thirty that afternoon that I got the chance to ask Jackie why she didn't want to go to the corn maze. She and I were alone in the kitchen, and the few patrons left in the dining room were finishing their meals.

"You didn't seem enthusiastic about visiting the corn maze." I put the lid on a container of chopped onions and avoided eye contact. I didn't want Jackie to feel like I was pressuring or criticizing her.

"I just think it's in poor taste for the Ostermanns to proceed as if nothing happened," she said. "I realize Ms. Pridemore wasn't family, but it was her land. The woman's funeral is tomorrow. Hosting a celebration two days later seems disrespectful. Don't you agree?"

"To an extent." I put the onions in the refrigerator. "But, one, I imagine the Ostermanns spent quite a bit of money designing the corn maze and everything. They probably can't afford to miss a weekend if they want to come out in the black."

"And what is *two*?"

I couldn't mistake the note of suspicion in her voice. "Two is that I want to know what—or who—killed Gladys Pridemore."

Jackie grasped my arm. "Has her death been ruled a homicide?"

"Right now, I believe the police are calling it a suspicious death and are investigating," I said.

"And you feel the need to stick your perky little nose into the investigation because...?"

"Because we found her, Jackie! And because whatever killed her could've harmed us too." I looked up into her dark blue eyes. "I want to know what caused that woman's death, don't you?"

"Yeah. Yeah, I guess I do." She sighed. "I'll go to the bonfire, but no way are you getting me to waste my time wandering lost in a stupid maze."

I grinned. "We'll see." I seriously doubted I'd be able to talk my stubborn cousin into going through the maze, but maybe Roger could.

Shelly came to the window between the kitchen and dining room. "Sheriff Billings is here to see you, Amy."

I thanked her, wiped my hands on a dish towel, and went out to greet the sheriff.

"Afternoon, Amy," he said.

"Hey, Sheriff. The special of the day was stuffed pepper casserole. Would you like to sample it?"

"No need. I love stuffed peppers, and I figure if you made it, it's bound to be good."

"I appreciate your vote of confidence." I went back into the kitchen and filled a plastic bowl with the remainder of the casserole. I returned to find Sheriff Billings sitting on a stool at the counter.

"Thank you." He spoke distractedly.

"Something on your mind?" I asked.

"Just Molly." He gave me a tight smile. "I'll be glad when she gets back home."

"I'm sure you will." I paused. "I understand Gladys Pridemore's funeral is tomorrow."

He nodded. "It is."

"Will you be attending?"

"I might stop in and pay my respects." He arched a brow. "What're you trying to beat out of the bushes, Ms. Flowers?"

His switch to formality had me thinking he'd put his guard up, and it made me feel defensive too.

"Ms. Pridemore's brother-in-law, Malcolm Pridemore, was here this morning," I said. "He wasn't the nicest person I've ever met." I shrugged. "But I imagine he's grieving."

"Yes...that sounds about right."

"He said he'd been hoping to buy Ms. Pridemore's property." In fact, I'd just about bet that he was the one who tried to get Ms. Pridemore to renege on her rent-to-own agreement with the Ostermanns. I smiled slightly. "It'll be interesting to see if Mr. Pridemore tries to convince the Ostermanns to sell." I shrugged. "Oh, well. Would you like some pie or cake?"

"I wouldn't say no to a slice of that apple pie."

"Would you prefer that here *a la mode*? Or to go?"

"To go, please, Nancy...I mean *Amy*."

Of course, I caught his sarcastic Nancy Drew reference, but I ignored it and cut the sheriff a generous slice of pie.

At home that afternoon, I took my laptop out onto the front porch and sat on the swing. Even though one of the wicker rockers might have been the better choice for the laptop's stability, the side of the porch with the swing was shadier and allowed me better screen visibility.

I opened a search engine and typed the name MALCOLM PRIDEMORE into the search bar. Results for other people with similar names were returned, but there was nothing relevant to the prickly man I'd met at the café this morning. Malcolm Pridemore wasn't even mentioned in connection with Gladys Pridemore's funeral. I thought perhaps he'd be listed as a survivor but Ms. Pridemore's obituary didn't name any. It stated only that she was preceded in death by her husband Lawrence. That was it. No siblings, no children, no "special friends." How sad.

I considered attending the funeral, but the service was tomorrow mid-morning—our busiest time of day—and I hadn't made the necessary arrangements with Jackie or other members of my staff. Surely, the Ostermanns would attend the ceremony. Wouldn't they?

I closed the laptop. There was a pound cake in the freezer that might just help me get some answers.

Gayle Leeson

"Come on in!" Nadine Ostermann called when I knocked on the door of the mobile home.

I opened the door and found myself in a surprisingly spacious living room. Nadine emerged from the doorway to the kitchen and motioned me back.

"I'm making spaghetti squash." Nadine wore a short-sleeved t-shirt dress, woven brown sandals, and a white apron. Her maple-colored hair had been pulled up into a bun on top of her head.

I followed Nadine into the kitchen. After the relative neatness of the living room, I was shocked to find that the table and countertops were cluttered to capacity. Not knowing where I should put the cake, I continued to hold onto it.

"Thank you," Nadine said, taking the cake and placing it in the refrigerator. "Big Harry and Harry Junior will be tickled to death."

"I'm glad."

Nadine motioned toward the table. "Clear you off a chair and sit down. I'll have this squash in the oven in a couple of minutes, and we can chat."

I felt uncomfortable doing so, but I picked up a stack of magazines and placed them on the table atop another stack of magazines. Beneath the periodicals in the chair were a pair of binoculars. I noticed that the initials *LP* had been sewn into the strap. I carefully balanced the binoculars atop thc magazines. At the bottom of the chair, there was a seed catalog. I moved it onto another chair that contained a mound of mail, and then I sat.

While I'd been finding the chair cushion, Nadine had been cutting the squash into rings with an electric knife. Now she unplugged the knife and began removing the seeds with a spoon. "Sorry about that. That woman on television who hates clutter would have a field day with my kitchen, wouldn't she?"

I gave a little laugh. "I don't think anybody is as neat as that woman."

"I know there's more than one way to make spaghetti squash, Amy. How do you make yours?"

"It depends on how much time I have, but I like to cut the squash in half and roast it cut-side down."

"Cut-side down, eh? Why's that?"

"The moisture ends up on the pan rather than in the squash," I said.

"Huh. I'll have to try that next time." After Nadine had put the squash in the oven, she cleared off the chair opposite me and sat down. "I think it's wonderful that you're hosting the farmers' market every Saturday for the next few weeks. Big Harry and I enjoyed being there, meeting people, selling our produce, and getting exposure for the corn maze. It's awful that the day ended in tragedy, but the farmers' market was nothing short of a blessing to us."

"I wish I'd been able to shop. I underestimated how hectic the café would be." I shrugged. "Hopefully, I'll have more time this coming Saturday to look around."

"Well, you can shop from us now, if you'd like," Nadine said.

"I don't want to put you to any trouble." I nodded toward the oven. "And I certainly don't want to cause you to burn your squash."

"All right, but you're getting first dibs on Saturday morning even if I have to go inside and oversee the café while you shop."

I laughed. "Deal."

"Even though we've been in Winter Garden for a little less than a year, we've been *here* on the farm almost all the time. We haven't been out in the community like we were on Saturday. I enjoy farm life, but it can get lonely."

"I imagine so," I said. "I really should be going. I wanted to come by and bring you the cake and…well, maybe…give you a warning."

Nadine stiffened. "About what?"

"Malcolm Pridemore."

"Oh, him." She relaxed back into her seat. "We've had the…I can't say *the pleasure* because it sure wasn't."

I lifted my hands. "You don't have to tell me. I had the displeasure myself this morning."

"Isn't he a piece of work?" she asked.

"That's putting it mildly. He told me up front that if his breakfast wasn't prepared to his exact specifications, he'd refuse to pay."

Nadine gaped. "What did you do?"

"I did my best to have the food meet his exacting standards. Then, I turned him over to Jackie—my cousin—who was working the register at the time. He tried to get her to reduce the price because his bacon wasn't quite as crispy as he'd have liked."

"What did Jackie do? Did she give him the discount?"

"Nope." I grinned. "She told him, 'you ate it, you pay for it.'"

Nadine slapped the table and laughed. "I love it. Maybe I can hire her to deal with him the next time the old grouch comes around here."

"Has he been pestering you and Harry to sell him the land?" I asked.

She raised her brows. "He sure has. How'd you know?"

"He was talking about wanting to buy his sister-in-law's property while he was in the café today."

"He was here yesterday. Poor Ms. Pridemore isn't even in the ground yet, and he's trying to get his hands on her land." Nadine shook her head. "The will hasn't been read or anything. I don't know how he thinks we can possibly do anything right now."

"Did Malcolm Pridemore visit his sister-in-law often?"

"Never. As far as we know, the first time that man had darkened her door in the time that we've been here was two weeks ago."

Ryan pulled into my driveway right after I did. He'd been traveling in the opposite direction—coming from town—and he stopped and waved me across in front of him before parking his police cruiser behind my yellow Bug.

I hopped out of the car with a wide smile on my face. "This is a nice surprise. Did you stop by to remind me of how handsome you look in your uniform, or are you here on official business?"

Instead of the cute remark I was expecting, Ryan said, "I simply wanted to stop by and see you for a minute."

He was serious. He was standing stiff as a board rather than leaning casually against his car. He hadn't kissed me hello. Something was wrong. I quickly looked toward the big house.

"Ryan, what is it? What's wrong?"

"Nothing. Everything's fine."

I turned back to examine his face.

"Sheriff Billings is concerned about you," he said. "And after seeing you arrive from the direction of Gladys Pridemore's house, so am I."

"I took a pound cake to Nadine Ostermann and expressed my sympathy." I crossed my arms over my chest. "Since when is my having good manners something for you to be worried about?"

"Good manners are one thing. Sleuthing is something else entirely."

I could feel the color rising in my face. "Following your boss's orders to tell me to stop sticking my nose into his investigation is one thing. Agreeing with him is something else entirely."

"I didn't say I agreed with him."

For some reason, Ryan's calm, rational "Deputy Hall" voice irritated me more than if he'd shouted.

"You didn't have to say it," I said. "I asked Sheriff Billings about Gladys Pridemore's funeral when he was in the café this afternoon because I was saddened that the only family member she might have there is a brother-in-law who came to Winter Garden for the sole purpose of getting his hands on her land."

Ryan started to speak, but I held up my hand.

"I even considered going to her funeral myself because I wanted there to be someone there. From the way her obituary reads, the poor woman had no one," I said.

He put his hands on his hips. "From everything we've learned during this investigation, solitary is precisely the way Gladys Pridemore wanted to be. The woman wasn't the sweet, little old lady you're imagining."

"Whatever." I fluttered my hand. "You can go back and tell your boss that I apologize for taking an interest in the woman Jackie and I found unconscious three days ago."

I turned to walk toward the house, and Ryan fell into step beside me.

"Look, I'm sorry," he said. "It's just...I know how you are."

"Right." I refused to look at him. No way would I let him see the tears glittering in my eyes. "Goodnight."

"Amy—"

The police radio squawked.

"I think that's your cue to go," I said.

Waiting until after I heard Ryan's car drive away, I walked through the house, out the back door, and stormed up to the big house. Mom and Aunt Bess would surely commiserate with me. Little did I know I was about to be in for the second rude awakening of my day.

"I agree with Ryan and Sheriff Billings," Mom said, after I'd told her all about my argument with Ryan. "You have no business trying to figure out what caused Gladys Pridemore's death. You're treating it as if she were murdered, but you have no proof of that."

"Mom, I can *feel* it. And the police aren't coming right out and saying so, but they believe it too." I looked at Aunt Bess.

She screwed up her mouth and said, "As much as I'd like to have something new to add to my *Crime Scenes* board, it appears to me that Gladys just fell over dead. I mean, they didn't find poison in her body or anything, did they?"

"I don't think the autopsy report has come back yet, but I'm positive it will show that Ms. Pridemore was murdered." I huffed. "But that's beside the point. I truly do feel sorry for Ms. Pridemore because she seemed to be so alone. According to Ryan, she preferred it that way. But come on—who wants to be alone?"

Aunt Bess shook her head. "I already told you how she was in school...acting like she was better than everybody else. Maybe—other than her husband—she never found anybody else who she felt was good enough to hang around with...the old thing."

My jaw dropped. "Aunt Bess!"

"I meant to say, bless her heart." She lifted her chin.

I decided my best bet was to change the subject. "Jackie, Sarah, and I are planning a fantastic girls' night for us tomorrow, Aunt Bess. We're going to be playing cards and—"

"What are we eating?" she asked.

"I thought we'd have pigs in a blanket, fried pickles, slow cooker party mix—if Mom will man the slow cooker for me tomorrow."

"Of course, I—" Mom began.

"You'd better believe she will," Aunt Bess interrupted. "You just bring it up here before you go to work in the morning and tell her what to do." She gave Mom a reproachful glare. "That's the least she can do after making plans to go out with a man none of us have ever even laid eyes on and leaving me here to fend for myself."

I opened my mouth to remind Aunt Bess that she wasn't having to fend for herself and that she was the only one of us who hadn't met Dr. Bennett yet, but Mom gave a slight shake of her head. She was right. Best not to argue with Aunt Bess.

"What else are we having?" Aunt Bess asked.

"I thought we'd have a crudités platter and some cookies."

She clapped her hands together. "I do love cookies."

With a smile, I bent and kissed her cheek. "I know." I kissed Mom's cheek too, and then I told them goodnight and went home.

I'd left my phone on my kitchen counter before leaving out the back door to go up to the big house. When I checked it, I saw that I'd missed three calls from Ryan. He hadn't left any messages.

I texted him: "Let's please not argue. You were right. I'm really tired, so we'll talk tomorrow."

With a sigh, I plugged my phone into the charger and went to take a bath. I hoped everything would be all right between Ryan and me. He was truly the sweetest man I'd ever known. I didn't want a murder investigation to ruin our relationship.

Chapter Seven

When Homer arrived at the Down South Café for his sausage biscuit the next morning, he could see right away that something was off. As much as I hate to admit it, I was so distracted that I neglected to ask him to tell me his hero of the day.

I'd poured his coffee and was turning to go back into the kitchen to prepare his breakfast when he said, "My hero today is H. Jackson Brown, Jr., Amy."

I gave him a half smile and tried to pretend I was interested. "I'm sorry, I'm not familiar with the name."

"Mr. Brown wrote *Life's Little Instruction Book*. One of his quotes is, 'Don't forget, a person's greatest emotional need is to feel appreciated.' I truly appreciate you, Amy."

Unable to speak due to the knot that formed in my throat, I merely nodded. And despite my valiant attempt to hold them back, two fat tears rolled down my cheeks. I patted Homer's hand and ambled into the kitchen.

Safely tucked behind the closed door, I took a steadying breath and used a napkin to wipe my eyes. I went over to the sink and washed my hands before slipping on a pair of gloves and putting Homer's sausage patty on the grill.

Jackie burst through the door, blue eyes blazing. "What's going on?"

"I'm making Homer's sausage biscuit. What's going on with you?"

She crossed her arms. "You know what I'm talking about. I want to know why Homer is out there giving Ryan the third degree."

I nearly gave myself whiplash snapping my head around to look at Jackie. "Ryan's here?"

"Yeah, and Homer is about to challenge him to a duel or something. Tell me what's going on. Do I need to go kick Ryan's butt myself?"

"No." I looked up at the ceiling to stem the tears that threatened again.

"That's it. I'm going out there and—"

"Stop!" I caught her just before she got to the door. With her long legs, she had no trouble outpacing me.

Jackie turned and stared me down.

"Let me get Homer's sausage biscuit ready, and I'll tell you everything."

"All right." She returned with me to the grill, and I told her what had happened yesterday.

By the time I'd finished relating my version of the previous evening's events, Homer's biscuit was ready. I looked at Jackie and could tell she was struggling.

"You're with them, aren't you?" I asked. "You think Ryan, Mom, and Aunt Bess are right."

"Not necessarily. I'm always on your side—you know that. It's just that I'm not sure this battle is one worth fighting."

"It isn't. I came to that conclusion last night." I took a deep breath. "But I don't want to go out there and look like an idiot in front of everyone."

"Homer and Ryan are the only two patrons in the dining room right now," Jackie said.

"All right." I picked up the plate with Homer's biscuit.

Seeing that my hand was shaking, Jackie took the plate. "I've got the biscuit. You go make up with your man."

I hesitated.

"Go," she said firmly.

I walked ahead of her. My eyes locked on Ryan's, and then I quickly scanned the dining room to see that Jackie had been right—only he and Homer were in the dining room at the time.

As Jackie placed his biscuit in front of him, Homer elbowed Ryan in the ribs and said, "Remember what Mr. Brown said are the nine most important words of any family."

"I love you, you are beautiful, please forgive me."

Ryan rattled off the words mechanically, and I laughed.

He grinned. "I'm sorry, Amy. I didn't mean to—"

"*I'm* sorry. I overreacted to your concern."

Before Ryan could say anything else, Homer spoke up. "Let's put this whole ordeal behind us and eat."

"Good idea," I said with a smile.

After closing the café, I stayed behind to clean the doors and windows. Jackie had offered to stay and help, but I asked her to choose a cookie recipe from Aunt Bess's *Things I'd Like to Eat* board and either make the cookies or ensure we had all the ingredients at the big house to bake them later. She'd happily agreed to leave then.

I was alone. The front door was locked, and the CLOSED sign was in the window. Cleaning the windows was peaceful, mindless work that allowed my thoughts to wander.

I remembered how sweet Ryan had looked this morning when he'd recited those nine words essential to families. What were they again? *Forgive me.* No. *Please forgive me. You are beautiful.* That was six. *I love you.* Nine words. Yep, I'd say they were essential.

I love you. Ryan had never said those words to me before...and I hadn't said them to him either. Of course, I realized the only reason he'd said them this morning was because Homer had encouraged— practically *forced*—him to do so. It was a joke...an icebreaker. And it had worked. He'd made me laugh, and the tension between us had dissolved.

I didn't kid myself that Ryan was in love with me. We'd only known each other for a few months.

Still...I was falling for him. It would be wonderful to believe he felt the same way.

I heard a car door shut, and my first thought was that Sheriff Billings was running awfully late today. He hadn't been in for lunch either.

But it wasn't Sheriff Billings who was standing at the door. It was a diminutive woman wearing a black crepe dress, black shoes, and a black hat with a white ribbon band, and she was cupping her face against the glass to see inside.

I unlocked the door and stepped outside. "I'm sorry. The café is closed. Everyone has gone home except me, and I'm cleaning the windows."

"Oh, shucks." The woman's voice was reedy and tired sounding. "I was hoping to speak with the owner about setting up a booth at the farmers' market this coming Saturday."

"That's me," I said. "I'm the owner." I put out my hand. "Amy Flowers."

She delicately shook my hand. "Hilda Dinsmore. It's a pleasure to meet you. And I'm glad to see you're the kind of business owner who's not afraid to roll up your sleeves and do the tough stuff."

"Thank you." I opened the door. "Come on inside, and I'll get you a vendor form, Ms. Dinsmore."

"Call me Hilda," she said. "I suppose you could even call me *Hil* if you like. It's what my friends call me—what few I have left anyway."

Having no idea how to respond to that statement, I merely smiled and said I'd get her that form. I went over to the counter and took the form from the stack beneath the cash register. Hilda slowly followed and sat on one of the stools.

"Please don't think I'm batty...or morbid," she said as I handed her the vendor form and a pen. "I'm feeling sad today. I've been to my friend Gladys's funeral."

"Gladys Pridemore?" I asked.

"Yes. Did you know Gladys?"

"I didn't. In fact, the only time I ever spoke with her was last Saturday." I explained to Hilda Dinsmore that Ms. Pridemore had called and ordered some food and that Jackie and I had found her unconscious when we'd made the delivery. "I'm sorry we didn't get there sooner."

Hilda screwed up her tiny, lined face. "Gladys called here and ordered food? Gladys Pridemore did that?"

I nodded.

"For what?"

"For some sort of party she was having on Sunday," I said. "She told me she didn't cook very much anymore."

She scoffed. "I believe somebody was pulling your leg."

"No, I talked with Ms. Pridemore myself."

"And you're sure it was her?"

"I had no reason to believe otherwise. The caller identified herself as Gladys Pridemore, ordered food, and gave me her address," I said.

"What did she order?"

"Potato salad, deviled—"

"Stop right there," Hilda said. "Now I *know* someone was pranking you. Gladys Pridemore was deathly allergic to potatoes. She'd have never had them in her house. That's why Gladys always did her own cooking. She needed to know exactly what was in her food and where it had been prepared."

"You don't think she ordered the potato salad for her guests?"

Hilda shook her head. "She would have never taken that kind of chance. I don't know who called you, sweetie, but it wasn't Gladys Pridemore."

Apples and Alibis

After Hilda Dinsmore left, I finished cleaning the doors and windows. As I wiped down the glass, I contemplated what she'd told me. If it hadn't been Gladys Pridemore who'd called me on Saturday, then who was it? I concluded that it must've been Gladys's killer. But why would her killer call and order food? Was the call to provide a witness to testify that Gladys Pridemore was alive at the time? No, that didn't make sense. Ms. Pridemore was still alive when Jackie and I delivered the food, so, of course, she was still alive when I received the call.

Maybe the caller hadn't intended to *kill* Ms. Pridemore. Maybe she—or he—had merely intended to scare the woman and had ordered the food so that someone would find her in time to save her. But we *hadn't* arrived in time.

None of it made any sense. The cleaner my windows became the murkier my thoughts. Ms. Dinsmore had to be mistaken. Gladys Pridemore had to be the person who'd called the café and placed the order on Saturday.

Then why would she order a dish that could kill her?

I put away the cleaning supplies, locked the doors, and headed for the police station. I had to tell Ryan about my conversation with Hilda Dinsmore.

I parked outside the building that housed Winter Garden's post office, Chamber of Commerce, mayor's office, and police station. As I got out of my car, I saw Ivy Donaldson walking toward the parking lot.

I called to her and waved my arm.

"Hey, Amy." Ivy approached and waited for me on the sidewalk. "How are you?"

"Have you got a second?" I asked.

"I do." She jerked her head toward a bench on the grass to our left. "Would you like to sit down?"

"Yes, please."

Once we were seated, I told her about my visit with Hilda Dinsmore. "I was going to speak with Ryan about it, but he and Sheriff Billings already think I'm putting my nose where it doesn't belong. Still, I can't ignore how adamant Ms. Dinsmore was that my caller was not Gladys Pridemore."

"No, you can't," Ivy said, "and neither can I. But before you take this new development to Deputy

Hall, let me check to see if Gladys Pridemore did indeed have a potato allergy."

"How? Wouldn't the body have to be exhumed?"

Ivy shook her head. "I kept tissue, blood, and hair samples. I'll run the test tomorrow morning."

"Thank you."

"Just doing my job," she said, with a slight smile.

"Doing your job would be running the test for Sheriff Billings. This is going the extra mile."

"My job is doing whatever it takes to uncover the truth."

"Gladys Pridemore was murdered, wasn't she?" I asked.

"You know I can't comment on an ongoing investigation." She stood.

I also rose from the bench. "Can you at least let me know about the potato allergy?"

"Sure."

A sudden inspiration struck. "A few of us are having a girls' night in tonight. We'll be playing cards and enjoying some good food. I'd love for you to join us."

Ivy mulled this over for a moment. "At your house?"

"At my mom's house," I said. "It's the big house on the hill behind my place."

"Okay. I might stop by."

Although I'd wholeheartedly meant the invitation, I didn't expect Ivy to actually come to our girls' night. I was surprised and delighted when she did.

Ivy handed me a bottle of Moscato when I opened the front door. "Here's my contribution. I'm not much of a cook."

"Thank you. Come on into the dining room, and I'll introduce you to everybody."

Since Ivy had been to the café on occasion, she was familiar with Jackie. She also knew Sarah because one or two of her investigations had led her to cross paths with Sarah's boss, Billy Hancock. As for Aunt Bess, that woman's eyes lit up as soon as I told her that Ivy was a crime scene investigator.

Aunt Bess got up and moved a chair between herself and Jackie. "Here, Ivy. You come sit with me."

"Gee, thanks, Granny," Jackie said, with a wry grin.

"Oh, hush. I can talk with you anytime."

Jackie shook her head. "Why don't we fill our plates? I'm hungry."

Apples and Alibis

Jackie and I had set up the food buffet-style in the kitchen so the dining room table could accommodate our card playing. In addition to the pigs in blankets, the fried pickle slices, the crudites, and the party mix Mom had so faithfully tended today, we had diet cola brownies that Sarah had brought, oatmeal butterscotch cookies that Jackie had made, and chips and salsa I'd picked up at the grocery store. While everyone else began piling food onto their plates, I got out the wine glasses and the corkscrew.

When we had reconvened in the dining room, I asked, "Would we prefer to talk while we're eating, or would you rather play cards?"

Aunt Bess took it upon herself to answer for everyone when she announced, "We're not playing anything until Ivy has told me everything."

Ivy's lips tightened. "What would you like to know?"

"What's the most gruesome crime scene you've ever come across?"

"Granny! Not while we're eating!"

Ivy laughed. "Jackie's right, Bess. I can tell you about crime scenes later—with all the gory details."

"Oh, good. I've got a *Crime Scenes* board on Pinterest, you know."

"I didn't know that," Ivy said. "I'll have to check it out."

I noticed that Ivy had relaxed considerably once she'd realized Aunt Bess wasn't going to ask questions about her personal life. Was Ivy truly all about the job, or was there a reason she guarded her privacy so stringently?

"How about serial killers?" Aunt Bess asked. "We can talk about them as long as we don't get too graphic, can't we? I'd love to hear your thoughts on Nannie Doss."

"The name rings a bell, but I can't recall any particulars of her case," Ivy said.

Aunt Bess took a sip of her wine and then pushed her plate forward so she could talk with her hands and not get her sleeves in her food. "According to Murderpedia—"

"*Murderpedia?*" Jackie interrupted. "Is that a real thing?"

"Of course, it is. How would I know about it if it wasn't?"

I saw Ivy raise her napkin to her lips to hide a grin.

"As I was saying..." Aunt Bess's glare dared Jackie to interrupt again. "This Nannie Doss woman was called the Giggling Grandma because she couldn't talk about the murders she'd committed without laughing. Can you imagine anyone being so heartless?"

"Unfortunately, I can," Ivy said.

"Aunt Bess, don't you think you'd be better off reading about people other than serial killers?" I shuddered. "You're going to give me nightmares just talking about it."

"And who would you have me read about?" she asked. "Homer's heroes?" She raised her sparse eyebrows. "Wait a minute—wasn't that a television program?"

"You're thinking of *Hogan's Heroes*," Sarah said, gesturing with her fork. "I remember my dad watching that show."

"How *is* your dad?" I wondered if Sarah realized how glad I was to be able to seamlessly change the subject.

Sarah and Ivy had gone home, Aunt Bess had gone to bed, and Jackie and I were cleaning up the kitchen.

"I didn't know you'd invited Ivy," Jackie said.

"I'm sorry I didn't mention it. It was a last-minute thing when I saw her earlier today, and I didn't dream she'd actually come." I placed a lid on the bowl of party mix. "I'm glad she did, though."

"Yeah. It was nice to get to know her a little."

"She's awfully private, isn't she," I asked. "I wonder what her story is?"

Jackie chuckled. "Have you moved on from Gladys Pridemore to Ivy Donaldson then?"

"Hardly." I told Jackie about Hilda Dinsmore's visit to the café. "I told Ivy about it, and she's going to run a test to see if Ms. Pridemore really was allergic to potatoes."

"And if she was?"

"Then I believe Ms. Dinsmore is right and that Gladys Pridemore didn't make that phone call," I said.

"But why would the killer call and impersonate Ms. Pridemore...*and* order food to be delivered to her house?" Jackie affected an old lady's voice. "Hello, I'm going to kill Gladys Pridemore, and it seems like hungry work to me. Could you bring some food over so I can have an after-murder snack?"

I laughed. "I agree. It makes no sense."

We stopped talking about Gladys Pridemore when we heard Mom's car drive up.

Chapter Eight

Dilly was our first customer on Thursday morning, but Walter wasn't with her. I hesitated to ask about him because I was afraid maybe they'd had a falling out. Jackie, however, had no such qualms.

"Hey, Dilly! Where's your sidekick this morning?"

"Walter had a doctor's appointment this morning and had to go there fasting, poor dear." Dilly shook her head. "I offered to bring him a biscuit, but he said he didn't want to be lumped in with the raccoon, so I'm making him dinner this evening."

Jackie laughed. "You look out for that raccoon! Walter should consider that an honor."

"You'd think so, wouldn't you?" Dilly looked over at me. "Amy, did you speak with Hilda Dinsmore yesterday?"

I exchanged a glance with Jackie. Surely Jackie remembered that it was Ms. Dinsmore who'd told me about Gladys Pridemore's potato allergy. "I did. She came in and asked for a vendor spot at the farmers' market."

"I warned Hil that you might not have any openings," Dilly said.

"Oh, I'm sure we can make room for one more vendor," I said. "I gave her a form, she filled it out, and I told her I'd look forward to seeing her on Saturday."

"Good."

Jackie topped off Dilly's coffee cup. "Have you known Ms. Dinsmore long?"

"Practically all our lives. Why?"

"I just wondered how reliable she is—you know, about..." Jackie shrugged. "Setting up at the farmers' market...and all."

"Honey, if Hilda Dinsmore tells you something, you can bank on it." She frowned. "Have you had many people back out?"

"Not too many," I said, with a smile. "What can I get you this morning?"

While I was in the kitchen making Dilly's blueberry pancakes, Jackie came in to talk with me.

"I'm sorry I was so awkward about that whole is-Hilda-reliable thing," she said.

I waved Jackie's concerns away with my whisk. "Don't worry about it. I understand what you were doing, and I'm glad you asked. I am interested to see what Ivy learns about the potato allergy, though."

"Me, too. What did Aunt Jenna say about her date after I left last night?"

"Not a lot. I got the impression she had a terrific time, but she seemed a little guarded when I asked about it... I think she might be frightened that Dr. Bennett is too good to be true."

She groaned. "I'm afraid she might be right."

I followed Jackie's gaze out the window into the dining room where Dr. Bennett was arriving with Shelly.

"Please tell me it was a coincidence that they got here at the same time," I said, through gritted teeth.

"You want me to go out there and fire her for you?"

"No. We can't fire someone for flirting with my mom's maybe boyfriend...can we?"

"It's possible." She shrugged. "Virginia is an employment-at-will state. You don't have to have a valid reason to let someone go."

"I don't know about that, but I wouldn't fire Shelly for such a petty reason." I took my frustrations out on the pancake batter. "Besides, if Dr. Bennett is a player, I don't want him anywhere near my mom anyway."

Homer's hero of the day was Augustine "Og" Mandino, II, the bestselling author of *The Greatest Salesman in the World*. So, one would've thought Homer would be spouting sales advice, right? Wrong.

"Why are your eyes shooting daggers at Shelly today?" he whispered to me.

"It's nothing." I hadn't realized I'd been so obvious in my irritation with Shelly.

"Well, whatever it is, just remember this word of advice from Mr. Mandino. He said to treat everyone you meet as if that person were going to be dead by midnight."

"That's a bit extreme, isn't it?" I asked.

"Hear me out," Homer said. "If you—again, according to Mr. Mandino—extend to them all the care, kindness, and understanding you can muster without expecting any sort of reward, your life will never be the same again."

I nodded. "That's excellent advice."

"Could I have a refill on my coffee please?" he asked.

"Absolutely." I got him more dark roast coffee and then went into the kitchen to prepare his sausage biscuit.

As much as I admired the altruistic attitude of Homer and Mr. Mandino, I found it difficult to set aside my feelings and muster up much care and understanding toward either Shelly or Dr. Bennett. Although he'd greeted me with a cheery hello and a smile as big as Texas—like we were best friends or something—he'd still told Shelly he'd see her later when he left. And *she'd* said she was looking forward to it. Since I'd never known anyone to look forward to a doctor's appointment, I could only guess the two of them had a date. Did the man honestly mean to go out with my mother one evening and with Shelly the next?

I smashed my spatula down on Homer's sausage patty, and it hissed. Grease popped onto my arm as if to scold me for being so rough. I closed my eyes and took a deep breath. Wonder if Mr. Mandino had anything to say about lothario doctors?

Jackie came into the kitchen and handed me another order. "This is for Ivy."

I looked up. "Ivy's here?"

She nodded. "I'll take Homer's biscuit out." She plated the biscuit.

"Wait. Did Ivy say anything about the test? Or the potato allergy?"

"Not to me. She probably doesn't know that I know...you know?"

"I should come out there and talk with her," I said.

"No," Jackie said firmly. "You should prepare her breakfast and then speak with her privately when you bring it out."

"Of course. You're right. I don't want to call attention to her...to me...to the test—"

Jackie sat the plate down and took me by the shoulders. "Amy, get a grip. Why are you so freaked out?"

I sighed. "It's everything. Shelly and Dr. Bennett...and I don't want Mom to get hurt...and I'm afraid Ivy is getting ready to confirm that Gladys Pridemore was murdered..."

"Can you do anything about any of those things?"

"No. I guess not."

"Exactly. What you *can* do is prepare a delicious omelet with turkey breast, low-fat cheddar cheese, spinach, and peppers," she said.

"Yes." I nodded. "Yes, I can do that."

She gave me a quick hug.

"Jackie? Thanks."

"Anytime." She took Homer his biscuit.

After I'd prepared and plated Ivy's omelet, I took it out to her. She was sitting at a table by the window and was watching a cardinal that had just flown up into a nearby pine tree.

"I love cardinals," she said.

"They're beautiful birds." I sat her plate in front of her. "Do you need a refill on your coffee?"

"Not yet. Can you sit a second?"

I caught Jackie's eye, and she nodded. "Sure." I sat across from Ivy.

"Thank you for inviting me to your mom's house last night. I enjoyed it. Your aunt is a character."

"That's putting it mildly. You'll have to check out her Pinterest boards."

She chuckled. "I'll do that." She lowered her voice. "I ran the test this morning. Gladys Pridemore was allergic to potatoes and likely other members of the nightshade family."

"Nightshade? The poison?"

"Just because two plants are in the same plant family doesn't make them both poison. Most people eat potatoes all the time and never have any problem. But some people—Gladys Pridemore being one of them—have severe allergies," Ivy said. "In addition to potatoes, she likely had an allergy to tomatoes, eggplant, and peppers as well."

"Then Ms. Pridemore certainly wouldn't have ordered potato salad from the café."

"I'd imagine she'd have had to have been extremely careful with the ingredients in her food as well as where it was prepared. I doubt she ate out much."

I glanced around the dining room to make sure no one was listening to our hushed conversation before asking, "Do you think she was murdered then?"

"I've had a strong leaning in that direction before I ever found out about the potato allergy," she said. "But in light of this additional evidence, I need to bring Sheriff Billings up to speed. He'll probably want to question you and Jackie about the call."

"Thank you, Ivy."

"Just doing my job."

Sheriff Billings came in during the lunch rush and took a seat on the patio. He sat at the table farthest from the door even though he was the only person dining outside at the time. Jackie told me all of this when she came into the kitchen to give me his order for a burger and fries.

"I'll get started on his food," she said. "He asked to speak with you."

"All right." I slipped off my plastic gloves and went out the back door, rather than walking through the dining room.

Sheriff Billings started when I came around the side of the patio.

"Good thing I'm not a criminal mastermind," I said, with a laugh.

"It is. But then I knew that when I sat down here, or I wouldn't have left my back open like I did."

I nodded, and it dawned on me that most of the time the sheriff—and Ryan, for that matter—sat with his back to the wall.

He took a breath. "I'm sorry if I was the cause of any conflict between you and Deputy Hall."

"You weren't. In fact, you were both right—I shouldn't have been...sleuthing."

"I owe you an apology for that too. Had you not been sleuthing, we might not have an important clue in our investigation. Ivy has brought certain facts to my attention that makes me think Gladys Pridemore's death might be more suspicious than we'd originally thought."

"The phone call," I said.

"And the potato allergy." He held up an index finger. "That doesn't mean I want you meddling in my investigation in any shape, form, or fashion. But I would like to speak with you and Jackie later today about the phone call you received from the person claiming to be Gladys Pridemore on Saturday."

"I'll be happy to tell you everything I can remember."

"Not right now," he said. "I don't want to interfere with your work. I'll come back near closing time."

"The special of the day is turkey tetrazzini. I'll save you some if you'd like."

"I'd appreciate that, Amy. Yesterday I had pizza, and I paid for it with heartburn all night."

Apples and Alibis

As I walked around the patio toward the kitchen door, I noticed that Sheriff Billings had switched seats. He was now sitting with his back to the wall.

I'd no more than stepped back into the kitchen when Shelly popped her head through the kitchen window.

"HJ Ostermann is here to see you, Amy," she said, clipping an order onto the window.

I blew out a breath and looked at Jackie.

"Go." Jackie jerked her head toward the dining room. "I've got this."

"I'll hurry back as quickly as I can. Sheriff Billings said he'll be back around closing time to talk with us about the phone call." I went into the dining room and looked around.

HJ Ostermann raised a hand and waved me over. I was glad. I wasn't as familiar with him as I was with his parents, and I wasn't sure I could've picked him out of the crowd.

"Hi, Amy." He gestured toward an attractive woman sitting to his right. "This is Fran."

"Hello."

"We wondered if we could put up a flyer here about the corn maze," HJ said. "We didn't do as well our first week as we'd hoped. Maybe it was because it

{ 133 }

was opening weekend and people wanted to get feedback before trying it out."

"Maybe it was because people were put off by that old lady's death," Fran said.

Before I could respond to HJ's request to put up a flyer, a man with long, wavy cinnamon- colored hair walked over to the table.

"Dudes!" he exclaimed.

"Scott!" HJ got up and hugged the man. "Have a seat, bro."

Scott pulled out a chair, sat, and winked at me. "Got any lemonade?"

"Yes, we do." I turned to go back to the kitchen. As far as I was concerned, Shelly could bring winky-Scott his lemonade, and I'd simply sidestep HJ's request to put up a corn maze flyer. It wasn't that I *didn't* want to help spread the word about the corn maze, but these three had put me off, especially Fran with her snarky comment about the *old lady's death*. How disrespectful could she be?

"Amy, wait," HJ said. "May I put up the flyer?"

"Leave it at the register, and I'll tack it up before I leave today," I said.

"Thanks. I appreciate that."

"Dude, wait—is this chick the manager or something?" Scott asked.

I raised my chin. "I own the Down South Café. Why?"

"I'm looking for work," he said. "I'm an actor, so I'm totally good around people, you know? And I've waited tables before. I can do handyman work—"

"That's right," HJ interrupted. "You made my mom some shelves, didn't you?"

"They're not finished yet," Scott said. "I'm still working on them." He turned his attention back to Amy. "So, if you need any help, I'm your man."

"We're fully staffed right now, but I'll keep you in mind," I said.

"Awesome." Scott gave me a wide grin.

I was happy to reclaim my place at the grill.

Jackie opened the door to the dining room and then stepped back into the kitchen. "Who's the pretty boy with the long hair who seems to be having the time of his life?"

I rolled my eyes. "Dude, that's like Scott, you know? And he's awesome and looking for work, and if we need any help, he's our man." I gave her an exaggerated wink.

Jackie was laughing as she walked out into the dining room. I was smiling too.

True to his word, Sheriff Billings returned at closing time. I'd already boxed up the remaining turkey tetrazzini for him, and he asked for a slice of chocolate cake to go with it.

Since Jackie had plans with Roger, Sheriff Billings talked with her first. He took her out onto the patio, while Luis and I refilled the napkin dispensers in the dining room.

Luis and I finished our job before the sheriff and Jackie finished their talk. I gave the young man some cookies to take home and told him to have a good evening.

While I waited, I absently wiped the counter down again and tried to remember anything unusual about Saturday's call...other than the fact that a person with whom I'd never spoken had called and insisted that the Down South Café deliver food to her late that afternoon.

Jackie came through from the patio, grabbed her purse, and told me she'd talk with me later.

Sheriff Billings followed Jackie into the dining room, sat at the counter, and took out a notebook. "Tell me everything you can remember about the call that came in on Saturday."

"Honestly, the only strange thing about it is that the caller begged us to deliver the food," I said. "I explained to her—at least, I *think* it was a her, but, of course, I thought I was speaking with Gladys Pridemore so the voice might've been disguised... Anyway, I said we don't deliver. We have carry-out orders, but we don't have the resources to offer a delivery service."

"What did the caller say to that?"

"She continued to be adamant that she needed the food and had no way of getting it if it wasn't delivered. She offered to pay extra."

"Is that when you capitulated?" Sheriff Billings asked.

"No. What made me give in was thinking about Aunt Bess. I wouldn't want my great-aunt to be without the food she wanted, nor would I want her out on the road endangering herself and everyone else in the vicinity."

"Do you recall any distinguishing characteristics of the voice itself?"

"No. We were busier than usual on Saturday due to the farmers' market, and I was in a hurry to get the caller off the phone so I could get back to work."

Sheriff Billings was writing in his notebook.

"That's the other thing, though," I said. "Gladys Pridemore's tenants—the Ostermanns—were here at the farmers' market. They could've taken her the food."

He looked up from his notes. "So, either the caller didn't realize that, or they thought *you* wouldn't realize that."

"I didn't. It was Jackie who pointed out that fact to me. We even tried to catch the Ostermanns so they could take the food, but they'd left already."

"Interesting." He closed the notebook and returned it to his shirt pocket. "I'll let you know if I have additional questions, and I trust you'll get in touch if you think of anything else?"

"Of course."

"Go ahead and lock up. I'll hang around until you leave."

Sheriff Billings went along behind me, ensuring that the doors were properly secured. Then he walked me to my car. For some reason, his protectiveness sent a chill down my spine. Did the sheriff know something he wasn't telling me?

Chapter Nine

I was relaxing in front of the television when Mom called. I'd heard her car go out only a few minutes before, and I answered the phone absentmindedly. I figured she was going to the store and was calling to ask if I needed anything. I was, therefore, shocked by the panic I heard in her voice.

"Amy, I need your help."

"What happened? Is it Aunt Bess?"

"Yes! She took off in my car!"

"She *what*?" Aunt Bess hadn't driven in nearly a decade. To imagine her behind the wheel of Mom's SUV was a terrifying thought. What on earth had possessed her to take off on her own—especially this close to dark?

"Come get me," Mom was saying. "We've got to find her."

"I'll be right there." I ended the call, turned off the TV, and slipped on my shoes. I grabbed my purse and keys on the way out the door.

As I sped up the driveway, I called Jackie. I knew she and Roger had planned to go to a concert but thinking—or *knowing*—Jackie needed her would certainly compel Aunt Bess to leave the house with no warning and without waiting for Mom to join her.

Jackie didn't answer. Either she'd silenced her phone or...I didn't want to think about the *or*.

Mom was standing on the porch. It was beginning to get dark, and she'd turned on the porch light. She sprinted to the car and got in.

"Have you tried to call Aunt Bess?" I asked.

"No. I don't want her distracted while she's driving. She's dangerous enough without my adding a ringing phone to the mix."

"You don't think something has happened to Jackie, do you?"

"I don't know," she said. "Your guess is as good as mine...as good as anyone's, as far as whatever is in Aunt Bess's head is concerned."

"What were you doing when she left?"

"Don't blame this on me." She snapped her seat-belt closed.

"I'm not trying to lay blame, Mom. I'm trying to figure out what happened." I supposed Mom was being so defensive with me because she blamed herself.

"Clark called me, and I went upstairs to check my calendar." She sighed. "I thought it would be fine. Even before Aunt Bess stopped driving, she wouldn't have taken my car without permission."

"Well, the main thing now is to find her." We were at the end of the driveway, and I looked at Mom. "Which way?"

She shook her head. "I don't know."

"Let's start with Jackie's apartment," I said.

Jackie's apartment was dark when we got there, and Mom's car wasn't in the parking lot. Mom went to knock on the door while I tried again to reach Jackie by phone. Still no answer.

Mom's hands were trembling when she got back in the car. "If something had happened to Jackie, Roger would have called us."

Unless, of course, something had happened to both of them. I didn't give voice to that thought.

"What should we do next?" Mom asked me.

"I'm calling Ryan."

Gayle Leeson

I'd barely gotten the words out of my mouth when he called me.

"Ryan?" I heard the incredulity and fear in my voice.

"Hi." He sounded calm...even like he was trying not to laugh. "Sheriff Billings wants to know why your Aunt Bess is at our crime scene."

"Crime scene?" I echoed.

"Yeah. There's been a small fire at the Pridemore house," Ryan said. "Aunt Bess is here taking pictures for all she's worth."

I let out a sigh of relief. "Mom and I are on our way."

Aunt Bess was getting a selfie with a handsome fireman when Mom and I arrived. After taking the photo, he handed her back the phone and kissed her cheek.

"I'm gonna make you famous!" Aunt Bess called to him as he rejoined his crew.

He lifted a hand in acknowledgment.

Mom took Aunt Bess by the arm. "You nearly scared us to death. What were you thinking?"

Aunt Bess jerked her arm away. "I was thinking I could get some excellent shots for my *Crime Scene* board—and I have too. It's gonna be *lit*. Wait and see."

"You took my car without my permission."

Mom was speaking through gritted teeth, and it seemed to me that Aunt Bess and I had somehow switched places like they do in one of those movies like *Freaky Friday*. I could recall Mom giving me this same lecture—and same murderous glare—not long before Nana had bought me my Bug. I tried to lighten the mood.

"Are you going to use that photo of you and the cute fireman?" I asked Aunt Bess.

She smiled. "Of course! I tried to get him to pick me up—you know, to make it appear he was saving me—but he was afraid he'd hurt me." She scoffed. "I'm not some delicate flower."

"I don't appreciate the two of you changing the subject," Mom said, hands anchored to her hips and nostrils flaring. "Aunt Bess, you took my car and left the house without my knowledge."

"I told you where I was going," Aunt Bess said. "If you were upstairs talking to your new lover boy and couldn't hear me, that's not my fault."

"How did you know the Pridemore house was on fire?" I asked.

"Somebody heard it on the scanner and posted it on social media." She scratched the side of her face. "I need me one of those scanners. I nearly didn't get here in time to get any good shots of the house."

Mom closed her eyes and pinched the bridge of her nose.

I could see both sides here. Like Mom, I'd been terrified at the thought of Aunt Bess racing off...in an SUV...behind the wheel...for reasons we couldn't fathom. But Aunt Bess was focused on her goal...and she loved her Pinterest boards...and she did claim to have told Mom...although I wouldn't have put it past Aunt Bess to have whispered so she could say she technically told her.

"Oh, there's Ivy," Aunt Bess said. "I need to go get an action shot of her."

Mom sighed. "I'm going home. Wrangle that woman out of here as quickly as you can. Or not. Whatever. I'm going to take a bath and have a glass of wine."

I watched her stalk off to her car. I started when I felt a hand on my shoulder.

"Sorry," Ryan said. "Your mom looks furious."

"She is. I don't think it'll be as easy for her to ground Aunt Bess as it was for her to punish me the one time I took her car without permission."

He grinned. "I admire Aunt Bess's spunk."

"Something tells me your boss doesn't find my great-aunt's spunk all that admirable at the moment."

"He does not. He's ready for her to leave."

"I'll see what I can do," I said. "What happened here anyway?"

"It's too soon to say. The fire was contained, so hopefully, there's not a lot of damage."

Before I could go in search of Aunt Bess, Sheriff Billings brought her to me.

"Amy," he said, "good timing." He took Aunt Bess gently but firmly by the shoulders and propelled her forward. "Good evening, ladies. Hall, I need you with me."

"I'll call your office for a statement," Aunt Bess said over her shoulder to Sheriff Billings. She shook her head at me. "You had to go and get caught talking to your boyfriend and ruin the investigating for both of us, didn't you?"

Ryan called me a couple of hours later. He said he was doing paperwork.

"Has the fire died down?" I asked.

"It has at the Pridemore house. How about there?"

"Barely." I laughed slightly. "The embers are still glowing, so we're all being careful to avoid stoking any lingering flames. Mom and Aunt Bess have gone to their rooms for the evening, and I'm back home."

"I think your fire was worse than the one at the Pridemore house," he said, with a chuckle.

"Do you know what caused the Pridemore blaze?"

"No. Now that the flames have been completely extinguished, Ivy and the fire chief are looking for the point of origin."

"Was the damage as minimal as you'd hoped?" I asked.

"I believe so. It was completely confined to the basement, and there didn't appear to be any structural damage."

"That's a relief. It would be terrible for the Ostermanns to finally be able to reap the benefits of their rent-to-own agreement and then have the house burn down." I wondered what had—or would—become of Gladys Pridemore's belongings. "Are Mrs. Pridemore's things still in the home, or has someone come to pick them up?"

"As far as I know, Ms. Pridemore's possessions are still in the house pending the reading of the will." Ryan's tone had become somewhat guarded, as it always did when I asked about something pertaining to an active investigation.

Jackie's number popped up on my screen.

"Ryan, Jackie's calling, and I need to answer. May I call you back in a few minutes?"

"How about I call you back when I get this paperwork finished?" he asked.

"Sounds good. Thanks." I switched calls. "Jackie, hi."

"What's going on? I just turned my phone back on to see that I'd missed two calls from you."

"Everything is fine." I explained what had happened with Aunt Bess.

"Oh, good gravy. Granny steering a two-ton projectile is a nightmare going somewhere to happen." She expelled a breath. "Aunt Jenna has got to start hiding her keys."

"I believe she's aware of that fact now."

Jackie was quiet for a moment. "On the other hand, I can hardly wait to see those photos."

I laughed. "You and me both." I then asked Jackie about the concert. Once she'd given me all the details, we hung up.

After talking with Jackie, I went into the fancy room, got my laptop, and stretched out on the fainting couch. I didn't know whether Aunt Bess had uploaded her photos to the *Crime Scene* board yet, but given how excited she'd been about her adventure, I thought there was an excellent chance that she'd either done so or was in the process. Since I had Aunt Bess's Pinterest page bookmarked, I clicked the link and my screen filled with the 1940s pinup she used as her profile picture and a list of her boards. I opened *Crime Scenes.*

She'd been busy.

I smiled at the photo of Aunt Bess with the fireman. What a sweet guy to have taken time to accommodate an inquisitive elderly woman. I made a mental note to drop off some cookies at the fire station.

There was an image of Ivy, unaware she was being photographed. She was grimly looking straight ahead, thoroughly focused on her task. Ivy was such a serious person. She seemed to be constantly on the defensive. I wondered if she harbored some secret pain and, if so, how I might help.

Aunt Bess had taken some impressive shots of the Pridemore house, especially given the fact that they were taken using a cell phone. I was certain the firemen had kept her as far away from the blaze as they possibly could, so she'd apparently used her zoom feature in some instances to make her subjects appear closer. Unfortunately, that had resulted in some blurred images; but, overall, they were pretty good.

One photo showed a man running away. I clicked on the image and enlarged it, but the figure was especially blurry because the man was in motion. Still, something about the guy seemed vaguely familiar to me.

I exited the frame and examined the other photos Aunt Bess had taken at the Pridemore house. If she'd captured the man once, maybe she'd taken another—clearer—picture of him.

She had.

After carefully scrutinizing each of the photographs, I found one additional shot of the mystery man. His back was to the camera, and he was at the edge of the photo, but there was definitely something about him...something rang a bell in my head...triggered a memory...

Dude!

That was it! The hair, the build... Of course, I couldn't be certain, but I thought there was a strong possibility that this man was Scott, the actor HJ had introduced me to earlier today at the café.

I called Ryan.

"Hi, there," he said. "I was just about to call you."

"Do you think the fire at the Pridemore house was set deliberately?"

"We haven't got any reported findings yet. Why?"

"Because if it was," I said, "I believe Aunt Bess might have a photograph of your arsonist."

"Let me call Ivy and get her impressions on the fire. I'll call you right back."

Ryan called me back less than twenty minutes later.

"I've talked with Ivy," he said. "I'm on the way to pick you up. You and I are going to talk with her—off the record."

Off the record. That sounded exciting. I was possibly going to learn something that I, as a civilian wasn't supposed to know. I could understand Aunt Bess's fascination with being in the thick of things...especially if I could be in them with Ryan and Ivy by my side and in no danger whatsoever.

I was watching for Ryan when he pulled into my driveway. I hurried to the car, got in, and gave him a quick kiss.

"So, where does Ivy live?" I asked.

"I'm not sure. We're meeting her at a coffee shop in Abingdon."

"Oh."

"Don't sound so disappointed," he said, with a chuckle.

"I'd just like to know more about Ivy. She's an attractive woman. Is she single? Married? Divorced? Widowed? Does she have children?"

"I don't know the answer to any of those questions, and my advice to you is not to ask. Ivy is an extremely private person. At work, we talk about work. Period." He shrugged. "That's the way she wants it. I don't think I've ever heard her just pass the day with someone."

I suddenly felt privileged because Ivy had accepted my invitation to come to girls' night. Granted, she hadn't said anything of a personal nature while she was there, but she had appeared to enjoy herself. I didn't want to overstep my bounds, but I did want to know more about Ivy.

"Do you think she's been hurt in the past?" I asked Ryan.

"More than likely. Haven't we all?"

"I suppose so. There's just something haunted about her...don't you think?"

"No," he said. "I don't think about it. She's an excellent crime scene investigator. As a deputy, that's all I need to know."

I guess he was right. Ivy's personal life was no one's business but her own. But that didn't stop me from wanting to know about it.

When we arrived at the coffee shop, Ivy waved to us from a booth in the corner. There were no other patrons in that area of the shop, and I knew she'd chosen it to give us privacy.

"How are you?" I asked Ivy, as I sat across from her. "That couldn't have been good for you, inhaling that smoke."

"I wore a mask," she said.

"Right." I felt ridiculous. *Sure, she'd worn a mask, plus she hadn't been fighting the fire like the firefighters. I needed to get out of my own head. Ryan was right—I had to stop worrying about Ivy...her life...her happiness, or lack thereof.*

"Do you think we're dealing with an arsonist?" Ryan asked.

That's what we needed. No small talk. Straight to the point, talking about the job. But that couldn't *be all there was to Ivy's life. Could it?*

"I do. I can't make that official yet because the arson investigator who arrived on the scene hasn't submitted his report." Ivy sipped her coffee. "There were multiple points of origin, the presence of an accelerant, and the fire pretty much remained on the floor."

I frowned. "What do you mean—the fire remained on the floor?"

"One point of origin was near a heater," Ivy explained. "However, it was obvious the heater didn't short out and cause the fire. For one thing, no one is currently living in the Pridemore house to our knowledge. And, for another, with very few exceptions, accidental heater fires start at the floor and travel upward."

"Wow." I smiled. "You're really observant."

She shrugged. "It's my job. You said you thought your aunt photographed a suspect?"

"I do." I took my phone out of my purse, opened the Pinterest app, and showed Ivy the photos.

"Even if we enhance the photos, we're not going to be sure this is the person you think it is, Amy," Ivy said. "His face is turned away."

"He doesn't know that," I said.

Ryan grinned. "You both know there will be no living with Aunt Bess if she's responsible for our nabbing an arsonist, don't you?"

I laughed. "No matter the outcome, in her mind, she'll have solved the case...and she knew it all along."

Chapter Ten

When my alarm went off, I groaned and smacked the snooze button. I rarely take advantage of the snooze button because I know continuing to lie in bed will make me feel worse in the long run. But I hadn't slept well at all last night. Nana would've said I'd spent the hours scheming instead of dreaming, and that was exactly what I'd done.

I hadn't voiced my thoughts to Ryan or Ivy, but I'd gotten the idea while the three of us were sitting at the coffee shop—what if I invited Scott to join the Down South Café staff on an as-needed basis? I could truly use an extra pair of hands tomorrow during the farmers' market. And although it was unreasonable to expect him to confess to setting a fire in Gladys Pridemore's basement—if, in fact, he did—he might say something to someone to confirm that he was the person in Aunt Bess's photo. At that point, we could confront him...or, well, Ryan could.

The alarm sounded again. This time, Rory heard it and bounded into the bedroom to pounce on my chest. No more rest for me.

Luis was in the kitchen refilling condiment bottles, and I was readying the coffee pots when Jackie arrived.

"I need to ask your opinion on something," I said.

She put her purse behind the counter. "I've already told you, I'll go to the Pridemore house tonight, but I won't go through that stupid corn maze."

"It's not about the corn maze. It's about Scott. I'm thinking of asking him to work here tomorrow."

"Who's Scott?" she asked.

"The guy who was in here yesterday with HJ Ostermann."

"Dude?"

"That's the one," I confirmed. "I think he might've set the fire at the Pridemore house, and I'm hoping that if we talk with him, he might give something away."

"Or—and I'm going out on a limb here—if the guy is a pyromaniac, he might set fire to this place."

I pressed the button to make the French vanilla coffee brew. "That thought did cross my mind."

"It crossed your mind?" Jackie asked. "It pulled up a chair, got a snack, and made itself right at home in my mind."

I laughed. "Jackie, what reason could Scott possibly have for wanting to set the Down South Café on fire?"

"I don't know. What reason would he have for setting the Pridemore house on fire?"

"That's what I want to find out," I said.

"Amy, this is a bad idea."

"He'll be here one day...and that's *if* he accepts my offer to work tomorrow. You've got to admit we could use the help, and it's possible the man wound up in Aunt Bess's photograph because he simply happened to be on the property visiting the Ostermanns." I shrugged. "He's HJ's friend. Plus, I think he's making some shelves or something for Nadine."

Jackie held up her hands in mock surrender. "You're the boss."

I heard the door open and turned, expecting to see Dilly since Shelly was off today, and Donna wouldn't be in until ten. Instead, Malcolm Pridemore strolled in wearing a seersucker suit and carrying a silver-handled cane.

"A pleasant morning to you, miss," Mr. Pridemore said to Jackie as he took a seat at a table in the middle of the dining room. He caught my eye and nodded.

"Good morning," I said.

"May I start you off with some coffee?" Jackie asked.

"Please."

The man was much nicer this morning, but I still didn't trust him. Had he altered his behavior because he realized he'd acted like a jerk the last time he was here or was he trying to present a cordial façade to hide the fact that he'd killed Gladys Pridemore?

As Jackie got Mr. Pridemore's coffee, Dilly and Walter came in. The pair had on matching neon green t-shirts this morning.

"Here comes the sun," I said, with a smile.

"No chance of our losing each other in a crowd this way." Walter wagged his eyebrows. "If I lose my girl, I can ask people to help me find a beauty wearing the same shirt as me."

Dilly blushed and rolled her eyes. "Then you'd better hope I don't switch shirts with Dolly!"

"She's a looker, but she's not in it with you, my sweet," Walter told her.

"I take it you two are headed to Dollywood," Jackie said.

"We sure are." Dilly looked at Malcolm Pridemore. "Unlike you, sir. From the looks of that suit, you must be off to somewhere way more somber than Dollywood."

"My sister-in-law's will is being read this morning," Mr. Pridemore said.

"Oh, well. I'm sorry for your loss." Dilly brightened. "But I hope you get something good."

Walter shook with suppressed laughter as he led Dilly to a table. "This one is in rare form today."

"She sure is." Jackie brought the coffee pot over to their table after filling Mr. Pridemore's cup.

I went into the kitchen, wondering what exactly it meant for him that Gladys's will was being read today. Did he expect to receive a bequest? Or did Mr. Pridemore merely hope that Harry and Nadine Ostermann would sell to him as soon as they took possession of the property?

As I prepared the lunch special—a white fish Po-modoro dish designed by my friend Sommer Collier of *A Spicy Perspective* blog—I preheated the oven for cookies. I had the cookies on baking sheets ready to go into the oven as soon as I heard the click alerting me that the oven had reached the desired temperature. I needed to replenish the chocolate chip and oatmeal cookies anyway, and I wanted to make an assortment to take to the fire station after work.

I placed grouper fillets in a large skillet seasoned with basil-infused olive oil I'd bought at the Olive Oil Company in Abingdon. I remembered Sommer's caution about fish: "Never, ever buy the fish that has been thawed and sitting out in the display case all day." She'd advised that if I couldn't buy wild, fresh-caught fish, I should ask the person at the seafood counter for completely frozen fish fillets.

"You'd be proud of me, Sommer," I murmured to myself, as the fillets sizzled in the skillet.

I hoped either Scott or HJ would come in for lunch today so I could ask Scott if he'd work with us tomorrow. But since yesterday was the first time Scott had ever visited the café and HJ didn't come in often either, I knew I needed a better plan than hoping and waiting.

I flipped the fish fillets and heard the oven click. I glanced over to confirm that the temperature indicator light had gone off, and I slid the cookies into the oven. Then I phoned Nadine Ostermann.

"Hi, Nadine. This is Amy Flowers. Could you please tell me how to get in touch with HJ's friend Scott?"

"Scott? Why do you want to get in touch with him?"

Nadine sounded defensive.

"I can assure you I'm not trying to take him away from you," I said.

"What?"

"I know Scott works at the corn maze, and I don't want to interfere with that in the least...but if he'd be free to help out at the café during the farmers' market tomorrow, that would be fantastic."

"Oh," she said. "Right."

"When he was here yesterday with HJ, he told me he has experience as a server."

"Sure...yes." She gave a slight laugh. "Please excuse me, Amy. You caught me off guard. My mind is a million miles away today."

"I can imagine. I understand it wasn't a devastating fire, but it must've been terrifying nonetheless."

"It was," Nadine said. "And then we had the will reading this morning, and Malcolm Pridemore tried again to buy the place."

"He certainly is persistent."

"After the fire and everything, I'm about half tempted to try to talk Harry into selling." She sighed. "But then again I don't want to give Mr. Pridemore the satisfaction. As it is, he's going to keep us out of the house for as long as he possibly can."

"How can he do that?" I asked.

"He was named the executor of Ms. Pridemore's estate. We can't move in until he dispenses with all her personal property."

"But doesn't he have to do that within a reasonable amount of time?" I made a mental note to ask Sarah about the duties of an executor.

"I don't know." Nadine sounded tired. "I'll look up Scott's number, call him, and have him either give you a ring or come by the café. Will that be all right?"

"That'll be good. Thanks, Nadine."

I didn't hear from Scott until the end of the day when I was carrying the box of cookies to my car. He was parking a beat-up sedan that looked as if it had been pieced together from several different makes and models of vehicles.

"Amy!" he called when he got out of Frankenstein's monster mobile. "Need any help?"

"No, thank you. I'm fine." I pressed the button on my key fob and unlocked the Bug. I opened the passenger door and gingerly placed the box on the seat.

Scott closed the distance between us. "Nadine told me you were hoping I could help you out tomorrow."

"That's right." I turned back to face him. "Is there any way you could work here at the café from six tomorrow morning until three in the afternoon? If those times don't work out around your duties with the Ostermanns, then we—"

"No, I can make it work." He was frowning slightly.

I felt sorry for him. If the Frankenmobile was any indication, he needed the money. But he also needed a little rest between jobs.

Gayle Leeson

"I'm guessing you stay fairly late at the corn maze," I said. "If you could be here from nine a.m. until one p.m., that would really help."

"Our last group starts at ten o'clock, so I should get home around midnight," he said. "I can be here at eight in the morning and work until three if that's all right with you."

I hesitated. "I don't want to push you too hard."

"Please. I'm going through some stuff right now and need all the work I can get."

"Okay." I told him how much I could pay, and he seemed happy with the amount. Then I told him I needed to go. "I'm taking some cookies to the fire station before I go home. The crew was super nice to my Aunt Bess last night."

"Your aunt was involved in a fire?" Scott asked.

"Only because she put herself there. She learned about the incident at the Pridemore house and went there to take photographs." I watched him carefully, but he gave nothing away. "The firefighters were awfully sweet to her despite the fact that she had to have been in their way."

"Aw, I'm sure she wasn't. I believe they have to be careful not to let civilians get in harm's way."

"Right." I smiled. "She did get some awfully interesting shots."

"Cool." The drawing together of his eyebrows belied his nonchalant reaction.

"Is anything wrong?"

Scott took a step closer to me. I'd have moved backward if my legs weren't already against my car. "Can I confide something to you?"

I nodded.

"Between you and me, I believe somebody set that fire on purpose," he said. "And I'd bet dollars to doughnuts that the somebody who set it was Malcolm Pridemore."

"Really? Why would he do that? Nadine told me he'd already asked her and Harry to sell him the property. Why would he set fire to something he wants to own?"

"To make Mr. and Mrs. O sell, dude! The fire wasn't bad at all." He shook his hair out of his eyes. "The fire department had the blaze under control in a matter of minutes, and nothing important was damaged."

"Is that what the Ostermanns said?" I asked.

"It's what happened." He spread his hands. "I know because I was there."

Driving to the fire station, I considered what Scott had told me. He hadn't seen Malcolm Pridemore on the property, so was his shifting blame to Gladys's brother-in-law merely a way of trying to cover his own tracks? After all, Scott readily admitted he was on the property. Had I made him nervous with my talk of Aunt Bess's photos? Maybe he'd seen her there and had correctly guessed he'd show up in one or two of those captured images.

I parked the car in front of the firehouse, got out, and went around to the passenger side to get the cookies. A group of firefighters sat in a large open area reminiscent of a den or game room. There was a sectional sofa, a couple of mismatched chairs, a television, a ping pong table, and a jigsaw puzzle in progress on a coffee table.

When I approached the glass door, a man facing that direction hopped up from his chair and came to give me a hand.

He pushed open the door. "Hey, there. May I take that box?"

"Please." I gratefully relinquished the package.

"Whatever is in here sure does smell good."

I smiled. "It's an assortment of cookies. My aunt crashed your work at Gladys Pridemore's house yesterday evening, and I wanted to bring you a token of my appreciation for being so kind to her."

"You're Amy?" he asked.

I nodded. *How in the world does he know who I am?*

"Come on inside." He called to the others. "Hey, everybody, Bess's niece—the gal who owns the Down South Café—is here."

They know Aunt Bess?

They ushered me into the kitchen and gathered around the long wooden table where the man who opened the door for me had deposited the box of cookies.

A tall, thin woman took a peanut butter cookie from the box. "We love Bess. Her *Lord Have Mercy* board is the best."

"And...how do you know her?" I asked.

"She followed our Facebook page," said the man who'd brought in the box, helping himself to a chocolate chip cookie. "She'd comment on our posts, message us to commend us on our service to the community..."

"Oh, and she ordered pizzas for us one evening," the woman with the peanut butter cookie added.

"I'm glad she got some new pics for her *Crime Scenes* board," a young man said. "It was awfully sparse before."

I recognized him as the firefighter who'd taken a selfie with Aunt Bess.

"That photo of the two of you together is fantastic," I told him. "She got another interesting shot or two as well."

"Really?"

Although the selfie guy had asked the question, I noticed the entire group had stilled and was looking at me.

"Yeah. In one, you can see a man who appears to be running away from the house."

They looked at each other and then left the kitchen. I trailed after them. One opened a laptop, and the others gathered around his chair for a closer look.

Like me, the laptop operator had Aunt Bess's Pinterest page bookmarked. He clicked the *Crime Scenes* board and began examining the photographs. "Here." He enlarged the image. "Look familiar to any of you?"

"He did to me." I cleared my throat when the crew looked at me for clarification. "I thought he was this guy named Scott who came into the café with HJ Ostermann yesterday. In a roundabout way, I asked him about it. He admitted to being on the property but said he believes someone else—Malcolm Pridemore—set the fire."

"Did you believe him?" the laptop operator asked.

"I don't know." I lifted and dropped one shoulder in a half shrug. "I did offer him a few hours work at the café tomorrow so that, hopefully, I or one of my staff can find out more about him and what he knows about the fire."

Ms. Peanut Butter Cookie pressed her lips together and raised one hand to her throat. "Bess must be so proud of you."

Chapter Eleven

I'd previously planned to ask Mom to loan us her SUV for the excursion to the corn maze, but since John also had an SUV and volunteered to drive, I thought that was a better option. We were all in high spirits on the way there, but Jackie still vehemently refused to go through the corn maze.

"The rest of you have at it," she said. "I'll be sitting by the bonfire eating s'mores when you're finished. Or you can call me from inside the maze, and I'll ask someone to fish you out."

Roger volunteered to stay with Jackie.

Although the corn maze was designed to look like a tractor from the sky—as evidenced by the drone photographs the Ostermanns had commissioned—it just looked like a bunch of foggy paths between corn stalks from our perspective. Fog machines kept the ground spookily covered and helped hide the wires attached to animatronic spiders that jumped out at us as we entered the maze.

Within the maze, there were more creepy things, such as tombstones with hands that rose from graves. Some paths led to dead ends, and some led to more choices...which either led to even more dead ends or more choices. Navigating the labyrinth somehow wasn't as fun as I'd expected it to be.

John and Sarah were both analytical. John had a notepad and a pencil, with which he documented our every wrong turn so that we could go back and get on the correct path. To me, this made no sense whatsoever. We were still just as lost. The only way John's directions would help us was if we decided to go through the maze again...which I definitely did not want to do. On the other hand, if we got lost, the directions *could* lead us backward out of the network of paths.

At various points within the labyrinth, actors would pop up and either scare you or offer you a riddle to guide you along the way. I was fairly sure Scott was supposed to scare us since he popped out from behind a hay bale in a werewolf costume with his arms raised up over his head.

But when he saw us, he broke into a wide grin. "Amy! It's me—Scott!"

"Hi, Scott. How do you find your way out of here?" I asked.

"I just walk through the corn, dudes. If you get tired of following the maze, just start moving toward the outside."

"Right or left?" The corn stalks were higher than our heads. "How do you know where you'll come out?"

"You'll come out wherever you come out, Amy-girl. It'll be somewhere on this farm. Then just look around and get your bearings."

"Makes sense," Ryan said. "But we'd like to try it the old-fashioned way first."

"Cool. Go back and take the right turn and also take the next right," Scott said.

"Thanks." I smiled, relieved that those were two dead ends we wouldn't run up against.

"It's the least I can do." Scott gave us two thumbs-up. "See you tomorrow morning."

John dutifully recorded the two turns Scott had given us on his notepad.

Ryan waited until he was sure we were out of Scott's range of hearing to ask, "What did he mean by *see you tomorrow morning*? Is he helping the Ostermanns at the farmers' market?"

"Actually, he'll be helping me out in the café," I said. "But I don't think this is the time or place to discuss it. Why don't we talk about it once we get out of the maze?"

"Oh, we certainly will."

I knew that, like Jackie, Ryan would not be happy that a suspected arsonist would be helping out at the café. I wanted to put off any discussion about that for as long as possible.

After we finally made it through the corn maze, we went to the bonfire to find Jackie and Roger. John offered them his notes on how to get through the maze quickly and without facing any dead ends.

"Where's the fun in that?" Roger asked. "I might steal a kiss at one or two of those dead ends."

"No, you wouldn't," Sarah said. "They have actors jump out at you in most of them to try to scare you or to annoy you with some silly riddle."

"Why don't we get some ice cream?" Jackie suggested. "This fire has made my throat scratchy."

"Sounds good to me," John said. "Let's head for Abingdon."

Ryan and I remained quiet on the drive. When we arrived at the ice cream parlor, we decided to sit outside on the patio. Since it was a cool night, the six of us were the only people out there.

I'd hoped Ryan would wait until we were alone to bring up the issue of Scott working at the café tomorrow, but he didn't. Right there in front of everybody, he asked, "Now, Amy, would you like to tell us why you hired a suspected arsonist to work in your café?"

I blew out a breath. "It's only for tomorrow. I'm hoping he'll let something slip about the fire...or Ms. Pridemore's death."

Roger looked at Jackie. "Are you all right working with this guy?"

"I tried to talk Amy out of it," Jackie said. "But she knows what she's doing."

I appreciated the valiant effort, but I also knew Jackie wasn't as sure about me knowing what I was doing as she was trying to let on.

"I appreciate the vote of confidence." I smiled at Jackie. "And, in fact, Scott has already admitted to me that he was at the Pridemore house at the time of the fire."

Sarah's eyes widened. "He did?"

"He did. He caught up with me today in the parking lot of the Down South Café when I was on my way to deliver cookies to the firefighters who were so sweet to Aunt Bess last night," I said. "Scott said he was there and that he believes Malcolm Pridemore set the fire."

"Scott could be employing a classic defensive maneuver," John said. "He could be providing an alternative suspect to deflect suspicion."

"I agree." Roger wiped his mouth with a napkin. "Did he realize you believed he was there before he mentioned Malcolm Pridemore?"

"I don't know." I stirred my sundae with my spoon. "I told him Aunt Bess was there taking photographs and that I'd made cookies as a show of my appreciation for the fire crew's kindness to her. Scott then told me that he believed the fire was set deliberately by Malcolm Pridemore in an attempt to get the Ostermanns to sell the property to him."

"If Scott has evidence against Malcolm Pridemore, then he needs to go to the police," Sarah said.

"If he *did* have any evidence, he'd have come to us with it already," Ryan said. "I don't trust the guy. Either he's guessing or shifting blame, and I don't know why either of those scenarios would induce Amy to offer the man a job."

"He'll be working at the café for one day," I said. "And I'd made my decision about that before Scott ever confessed to me that he'd been at the Pridemore house at the time of the fire."

"As busy as we were last Saturday, what do you hope to learn from Scott in one day?" Jackie asked.

"Maybe nothing," I admitted. "But, at least, he'll be an extra pair of hands tomorrow. If we *are* as busy as we were last Saturday, we'll need all the help we can get."

On Saturday morning, the farmers' market proved to be even more of a draw than it had been the week before. Word had spread; and by eight a.m., the crowd circulating among the vendors had already doubled what it had been all day the previous week.

I waved to Madeline Carver, who was selling Landon Farms honey. She merely smiled, having both hands full and being unable to wave back.

I saw the Ostermanns selling produce like crazy, but Nadine waved me over.

"Amy! Get over here!" she called.

I went over and bought some tomatoes, apples, peppers, and a pumpkin from the Ostermanns. I then bought fresh eggs and cucumbers from another vendor. I didn't have time to stop at Ryan's mom's booth, but as I passed by, I told her I'd try to get back out later.

She gave me a cold shrug and turned to greet a couple of browsers.

I told myself she wasn't actually giving me the cold shoulder...that she was just busy. But a nagging feeling in my gut told me otherwise.

I hurried into the kitchen using the café's back door and began putting away the produce I'd bought. Jackie was working at the grill.

"I'll take over for you as soon as I get squared away," I told her.

"Don't worry about that," Jackie said. "It's going to take us both to keep our heads above water today."

Shelly appeared at the window between the kitchen and the dining room. She had a stack of orders for us. "Amy, that gorgeous man who was with HJ Ostermann the other day is here asking for you."

"That's Scott," I said. "Send him back."

"To the kitchen?" Shelly asked.

"Yes."

Scott entered the kitchen with his arms outstretched. I was glad to see he had his hair pulled back.

"Good morning! How can I help?" he asked.

"You'll need an apron and an order pad." I handed him one of each. "Oh, and a pen." I looked around frantically.

"By the register," Jackie said.

"I'll get it," he said. "If there's anything else you need, let me know. I'm a whiz at chopping."

"Good to know," I said.

"We might actually need a chopper soon," Jackie said. "It's going to be all the two of us can do to handle the grill."

At around ten-thirty that morning, Scott poked his head through the window into the kitchen.

"Guru Guy is here for his sausage biscuit," he said. "Told me there was no need to waste a sheet of paper on it."

"He's right," I said. "It'll be ready in a minute."

"Cool."

When I had Homer's sausage biscuit ready, I took it out to him. Scott was refilling Homer's coffee cup.

"Who's your hero today, Homer?" I asked.

"Les Brown," Homer said.

"Dude has some powerful words of wisdom," Scott said.

I frowned slightly. "Homer or Les Brown?"

"Exactly." Scott jabbed an index finger into the air and took the coffee pot around to see if other patrons needed a refill.

"New hire?" Homer asked.

"For today."

"I kinda like him." Homer poured creamer into his coffee.

I turned to go back to the kitchen but saw Ryan from the corner of my eye. He was striding toward the counter, and his mouth was set in a hard line.

"Hey," I said. "Coffee?"

"No. I need to get back outside in a second and try to pacify my mother."

"About what?" I glanced toward the door, but I couldn't see the vendors very well from where I was standing.

"When you agreed to allow Hilda Dinsmore to participate in the farmers' market, did you realize she sold the same type of merchandise as my mom?" Ryan asked.

"I don't think I even asked Ms. Dinsmore what she was selling. I mean, I'm sure I glanced at her registration form, but I didn't give it a lot of thought."

"Hilda and my mom go way back. I don't suppose you'd consider asking Ms. Dinsmore not to return next Saturday," he said quietly.

My jaw dropped. "You *are* kidding, right?"

"Yeah. I am." He sighed and ran his hand through his hair.

"Is it really that bad?"

As if in answer to my question, I heard a shriek of anger.

"There it is," Ryan said, as he turned and strode out of the café.

I followed close on his heels.

"You always have to act like you're so much better than everyone else, Michelle," Hilda Dinsmore was shouting at Ryan's mom.

Michelle, her russet red hair gleaming in the sun, leaned closer to Hilda's face. "I might not be better than everybody, but I *am* better than you!"

"Ha! You'd better be glad my arthritis is acting up today, or else I'd come across this table and slap you silly." Hilda raised her chin.

Given her wide stance and clenched fists, I thought Ms. Dinsmore did look ready to fight. I, for one, was glad her arthritis was acting up. But apparently, Ryan's mom was not.

"Oh, yeah?" Michelle scoffed. "You and what flock of old hens?"

"Ladies, please." Ryan stepped between his mother and Hilda Dinsmore's table.

"Uh-huh." Ms. Dinsmore snorted. "Good thing that boy of yours came to rescue you."

Michelle tried to push Ryan out of her way. "Let me at her."

"Mom, come on." His voice was quiet but firm.

Ms. Dinsmore hurled a blue hacky sack across the table at Michelle and hit her in the face. Michelle growled in frustration and somehow managed to reach around her son and flip Ms. Dinsmore's table over.

"I'll sue you for my damaged merchandise!" Ms. Dinsmore screeched.

"Like I'm going to miss *that* one-dollar bill. I'll have *you* arrested for assault." Michelle looked up at Ryan. "Go on. You saw her throw a projectile at me."

I stepped forward. "Ding, ding. That round is over. Please go back to your respective corners."

"Amy's right," Ryan said. "You weren't injured, Mom, and Ms. Dinsmore's merchandise appears to be intact. Why don't we go back to your table?"

With one last look of disdain at Hilda Dinsmore, Michelle said, "Fine."

I helped Ms. Dinsmore right her table before going back inside.

"What was that about?" Jackie asked as I went back into the kitchen.

"Ryan's mom and Hilda Dinsmore were scuffling in the parking lot."

A few minutes later, Shelly brought me a note. It was from Ryan.

I'm sorry. Are we still on for dinner?

I wrote back: *I'm game if you and your parents are.* I was afraid that Michelle might not want to be anywhere near me since I'd helped her archnemesis put her table back in order.

At the end of the day, I was disappointed to see that there wasn't much left in the bakery display case. Still, I don't think I was half as disenchanted as Oscar was. The young man had worked the register for us again, and his face fell when he saw that there were no cookies left.

I looked around at the remaining staff members. Shelly and Donna had both left already. Scott, Jackie, Oscar, and Luis remained.

"Could the four of you stick around for an extra job?" I asked.

Jackie tried to hide a smile, but she didn't have much success. She knew I was up to something. "What job is that?"

"Cookie and brownie tasting," I said. "No extra money, but while you wait, I'll grill some cheese sandwiches."

"I'll stay for a cheese sandwich," Scott said.

I explained to Scott that we normally divide what's left in the display case among the employees on Saturday. "But, as you can see, there's not much to divide today. I have some cookies in the freezer that are ready to bake, and I can have a batch of cola brownies ready to go into the oven in five minutes."

"You do that, and I'll make the grilled cheese sandwiches," Jackie said.

"Nah," I said. "Luis can help me. You stay out here and talk with Oscar and Scott. After today, I'm afraid neither of them will come back to work for us next week."

"All right." Jackie nodded, letting me know that she understood my reason for wanting her to stay behind and talk with Scott.

Later, after we'd had grilled cheese sandwiches and divided the cookies and brownies, I encouraged Scott, Luis, and Oscar to go on home.

"No way," Scott said. "You need our help cleaning up."

"I'll take care of it," I said. "You've all worked hard enough for one day." I went ahead and paid Oscar and Scott for their one day of work. Both agreed to work again next Saturday.

"Did you learn anything from Scott while Luis and I were making the sandwiches?" I asked Jackie after they'd left.

"Not much. He told Oscar and me that he'd moved to Abingdon from New Mexico a couple of months ago."

I frowned. "How in the world did he get from New Mexico to Abingdon?"

"I'm guessing it wasn't in that awful little car he drives." Jackie laughed. "That thing would have probably pooped out a little less than halfway. But, seriously, he said he moved here to be near his sister."

I wandered behind the counter and got some cleaning supplies.

"We can do that Monday morning," Jackie said. "If you're as tired as I am, it's all you can do to put one foot in front of the other."

"I am that tired. Want a drink?"

"Bring us a drink in a to-go cup so we don't have to worry about washing it. I'll settle for anything cold." She sat at the table we'd shared with Luis, Oscar, and Scott. "So, tell me about the fight in the parking lot. I figured a couple of the farmers were throwing punches, but you said it was Ryan's mom and another woman."

I brought us both a sweet tea and sat across from her. "I'm not sure who started the ruckus, but Ryan's mom and Hilda Dinsmore were both selling crocheted and knitted items. And it was obvious that the two of them have butted heads before. When I went outside, Ms. Dinsmore was accusing Michelle of thinking she was better than everybody."

"And then what? Give me the play by play."

"It all happened quickly. Ms. Dinsmore threw a crocheted hacky sack at Michelle—Ryan's mom—and then Michelle turned Ms. Dinsmore's table over. That's when Ryan managed to get his mom to go back to her booth, and I helped Ms. Dinsmore tidy up." I sipped my tea. "I didn't even realize what Hilda Dinsmore was selling or that she and Michelle Hall knew each other when she signed on as a vendor. She'd been to Gladys Pridemore's funeral, and I thought maybe she could tell me something pertinent about Ms. Pridemore." I expelled a long breath. "Contrary to what I'm sure Ryan and Sheriff Billings believe, I'm not trying to interfere in the investigation, Jackie. I only want some justice for that poor woman."

"I think you're still beating yourself up because we didn't get there in time to make a difference."

Closing my eyes momentarily, I said, "I didn't want to go at all."

"Yes, you did. If you hadn't, you wouldn't have agreed to do it." She sighed. "I'm the one who'd have told her no."

I opened my eyes to see Jackie running her fingertip back and forth along the edge of the table.

"We can't help what happened," I said. "It wasn't our fault. We didn't—" I faltered. "Wait...no one has ever actually said how Gladys was murdered. Was she poisoned?"

"I don't know." Jackie gave me a half grin. "But I've got a feeling you're going to find out."

I received a text message and looked down at my phone. "It's Ryan. He wants to know if he can pick me up for dinner at six."

"You were supposed to have dinner with his parents tonight, weren't you?"

I nodded.

"So, that's still on?" she asked.

"As far as I know."

She snorted. "Well, that should be fun."

When I went behind the counter to get my purse, I saw a watch with a broken band. I picked it up and showed it to Jackie. "Do you know anything about this watch?"

"Yeah. It's Scott's. He must've forgotten it."

"I'll drop it off at the Pridemore house," I said.

"Anything to weasel out of dinner with Ryan's parents, eh?"

"No, I'm still going." I shrugged. "I'm just not in a hurry to get there."

"What're we making for lunch tomorrow?"

I sighed. I wasn't ready to think about making lunch for Mom and Aunt Bess. I was still trying to get over making lunch for half the county. "How about a brunch-type menu?"

"Sure," Jackie said. "Eggs, ham rolls, hash brown casserole..."

"Maybe some mini quiches. Lots of fresh fruit."

"I know Granny needs the fruit, but we'd better have some chocolate fondue for her to dip her fruit into so she doesn't fuss."

I smiled. "That sounds really good."

"It does. Kinda makes me want it for dinner."

"Me, too. If I get stood up by Ryan, would you and Roger like to meet me at the big house for dinner?"

"You won't get stood up," she said.

"How do you know?"

She scoffed. "Because Ryan is crazy about you."

Chapter Twelve

Ryan called me while I was driving home.

"Hey," he said softly. "I'm sorry about my behavior earlier today. Mom was freaking out..and I'm not crazy about your having a suspected arsonist working in the café."

"Scott's a hard worker and friendly with everyone. You should've seen how kind he was to Luis's little brother Oscar today."

"You know who else was friendly?" Ryan's voice had taken on a slight edge now, and he didn't wait for me to answer his question. "Ted Bundy. Did you forget why you hired Scott?"

"No, and we did get more information from him," I said. "Jackie learned that he came here from New Mexico to be closer to his sister."

"My dad is looking forward to meeting you, and both my parents are eager to get to know you better."

I was glad Ryan had changed the subject, but I wasn't sure his mother was all that psyched to get to know me...especially since I'd been in cahoots with her enemy, Hilda Dinsmore. I hadn't realized I'd been in cahoots, nor that Hilda was Mrs. Hall's enemy, but that was beside the point.

Ryan suggested a steakhouse in Bristol. "Would that be all right with you?"

"That sounds great. I need to go home, feed the pets, and get ready. Would it be all right if I meet you there?"

"Sure, but I'd be happy to pick you up," he said.

"I know, but your dad has been out of town. If you go ahead and meet them, that'll give the two of you more time together." *And it'll give me more time to prepare.*

"All right. See you soon."

Rory came to greet me as soon as I walked through the front door. I picked him up and gave him a cuddle as Princess Eloise wound around my ankles.

After I fed the pets, I took extra care with my appearance. I chose a summery dress with a tiny floral print and paired it with a cropped denim jacket with the sleeves cuffed. Tan wedge espadrilles completed the look without making it appear I was trying too hard. I wore a dainty necklace my Nana had given me and pearl stud earrings. Then I spent twenty minutes applying my makeup to look "natural."

When I got into the car, the first thing I noticed was Scott's watch with the broken band lying on my passenger seat.

Rats! Why hadn't I remembered to take that by the Pridemore house earlier? Oh, well...

Upon arriving at the Pridemore property, I parked near the Ostermann's mobile home rather than in the designated corn maze parking area. I knew if I didn't, I could be blocked in half the night. If I was truly trying to weasel out of dinner with Ryan's parents as Jackie had suggested, that's where I'd have left the Bug. But I didn't. Which goes to show how badly I really did want to have dinner with Ryan's parents. Really.

I got out of the car, pocketed the watch and my keys, and went in search of Scott. I found him putting blocks of dry ice in small plastic trash cans with holes in them. They were attached with something that looked like dryer hose to fog machines.

Before I got close enough to call out to Scott, Nadine walked past him and pinched his butt. Scott ignored his employer, and I wondered if her harassment was a common occurrence.

"Scott!" I called.

He turned. "Whoa! Amy-licious! You look gorgeous."

"Thank you." I handed him his watch. "You forgot this at the café. I'm sorry about the band."

"Aw, that's all right. I have another at home." He put the watch in his pocket. "You didn't have to come all the way out here to drop it off."

"No problem. I'm heading to Bristol to have dinner with Ryan and his parents."

"Good luck with that," he said. "Moms always seem to like me. Dads? Not so much."

Lowering my voice, I said, "I...um...saw Nadine pinch you."

He nodded. "Yeah. She does stuff like that sometimes." He turned up one side of his mouth as if to say, *what're you gonna do?*

"Just to you or to other employees too?" I asked.

"I don't pay attention to what she does to anyone else."

"You don't have to take that, you know."

He patted my shoulder. "It's okay."

It wasn't okay. I brooded over how not okay it was all the way to the restaurant. Either Scott needed his job too badly to rock the boat and tell Nadine to stop objectifying him, or else he didn't mind her attention. It wasn't all right for men to subject women to that sort of behavior, and it wasn't all right if the roles were reversed either.

The restaurant parking lot was crowded, and people were lined up on the sidewalk waiting for a table. I found a space, parked, and checked my phone. Ryan had texted me that he and his parents had a table in the bar area.

I went inside and saw Ryan standing by a table, waving me over. I hurried over, and Ryan kissed my cheek.

"Amy, this is my dad, David," Ryan said. "And you already know my mom."

David rose to shake my hand, and I told him it was nice to meet him. He echoed the sentiment. I could now see which parent Ryan resembled. He looked nothing like his mother, but David Hall was an older version of his son. Both men had the same dark brown hair, although David's now held a smattering of gray. And both had a sparkle of mischief in their deep brown eyes.

Michelle Hall had russet red hair and hazel eyes, which held no warmth for me whatsoever. In fact, they were glowering at me at the moment.

Ryan squeezed my waist before we took our seats.

"We're lucky we got here when we did, or else we'd be standing out in the parking lot at the end of that very long line," Michelle said.

"That's true," I said.

"We went ahead and ordered an appetizer." Michelle took a sip of her drink.

"I hope you don't mind," David said.

"I don't care if anyone minds or not." Michelle's gaze bore into my eye sockets. "We're hungry."

I decided then and there that if this woman was waiting for an apology from me for being late, she'd be waiting from now on. I wasn't late. Ryan knew I was going to be a while getting ready. Granted, he didn't know I'd needed to stop by the Pridemore house, but that was information I felt no need to volunteer.

A waitress arrived and asked me what I'd like to drink.

"I'd like water with lime please," I said.

"Watching your figure?" Michelle asked. "That's smart."

I didn't take the bait.

"Guess who was at the farmers' market today?" Michelle asked David. Without waiting for a reply, she said, "Hilda Dinsmore."

David groaned. "It wasn't a repeat of the church fundraiser, was it? Please tell me you didn't create a ruckus."

Michelle huffed. "I did no such thing. She started it." She pushed back her chair. "If you'll excuse me, I need to go to the ladies' room."

As soon as Michelle was out of earshot, I asked, "What happened at the church fundraiser?"

"Michelle thought Hilda upstaged her because Hilda had her items priced lower and sold more pieces," David said. "They argued about it right there in front of God and everybody."

"Don't forget the shoving match," Ryan said.

David laughed. "I wanted to schedule a pay-per-view fight and call it—" He tried to make his voice sound like that of an announcer. "—Altercation at the Altar." Regular voice, "Or if you prefer—" Announcer voice, "Violence in the Vestibule."

"Instead, we end up with Fracas at the Farmers' Market," Ryan said.

"Maybe next week, we can sell tickets and call the match Throwdown Amongst the Turnips," I said with a grin. "But why is there such animosity between Michelle and Hilda Dinsmore?"

"Because Michelle wanted it to be obvious to everyone in the church that she'd made more money with her craft than Hilda had. Hilda's items were smaller and, I imagine, easier to make than Michelle's afghans." David took a drink of his iced tea. "So, Hilda sold more of her bookmarks and ornaments, but Michelle's afghans brought in more money for the church."

"Then why wasn't she happy?" I asked.

Both David and Ryan laughed.

"Because Michelle wanted it to be obvious to everyone that she'd made more money with her craft than Hilda had," David said. "The woman is as competitive as all get out."

"But it...it wasn't a competition," I said. "They were working together for a common goal."

"Try telling *her* that," Ryan said.

"To Michelle, everything is a competition." David's lips twitched. "We'd better hush. Here she comes."

"What did I miss?" Michelle asked as she sat back down.

Apples and Alibis

"Not a thing, dear." David nodded toward the waitress, who was approaching with their appetizer. "See? You're just in time."

I didn't partake of the stuffed mushrooms partly because I wasn't terribly hungry and partly because Michelle had made such a big deal out of the fact that the three of them were famished.

Michelle speared one and put it on the plate in front of her. "So, Ryan...how's Ivy?"

"She's fine," Ryan said.

Wanting to contribute to the conversation, I said, "Speaking of your coworkers, I believe Sheriff Billings will be thrilled to have Molly get back home."

"I'm sure he will be, but he'll undoubtedly miss your cooking." Ryan squeezed my hand.

"I hope he'll bring his wife to the café when she returns." I smiled. "I'd enjoy meeting her."

"Have you met Ivy Donaldson?" Michelle asked me.

"I have. Ivy's great."

"It doesn't bother you that she and Ryan dated?" Michelle watched to see if my expression would change. I tried to hold that smile, but I must've faltered just enough to clue her in. "Oh. You didn't know?" She looked at her son. "Oops. Sorry, darling. I hope I didn't open any cans of worms."

"Michelle, what're you talking about?" David demanded. "Ryan and Ivy didn't date."

Ryan shot his dad a look of gratitude. "Thanks, Dad." He looked at me. "Ivy and I went to a dinner together right after I was hired. Almost all our coworkers were there. Just because Ivy and I carpooled didn't make it a date."

"Oh. Sorry," Michelle murmured. "I guess I misunderstood. You spoke so highly of her that I got the impression it had been more than a business dinner."

"Ivy certainly is a fascinating person," I said. "Aunt Bess tried to learn all about Ivy's work when Ivy visited us on Wednesday evening."

"Ivy came to girls' night?" Ryan asked.

"Yes. I thought I told you about that."

"I don't think so," he said, "but you should realize Ivy doesn't socialize very much. She must really like you."

"Tell us more about you, Amy," David said.

Not quite knowing what to say, I told them about Nana leaving me some money to follow my dreams. "I bought the Down South Café, had it renovated, and the rest is history."

"Congratulations on all your hard work." David raised his tea glass in a toast.

"Thank you." I clinked my glass to his.

Ryan held up his glass and we also "clinked." Michelle ignored us.

"I hope that waitress comes back soon," she said. "I'm ready to order. I'm having the filet mignon with garlic butter and a loaded baked potato."

"That sounds good," Ryan said. "Amy, what're you having?"

"I'm considering the Parmesan crusted chicken."

"I think it's wonderful that you're so cautious about your diet," Michelle said. "Someone in your line of work could gain a lot of weight in a hurry if she weren't careful."

"Fortunately for me, no one in my family has ever had a weight problem," I said.

David sighed. "Michelle, would you please try to relax and enjoy the evening?"

Ryan and his dad shared a smile, but Michelle pouted throughout the meal.

For some reason, I woke up with Sheriff Billings on my mind. I called Mom and asked her if she thought it would be all right to invite him for lunch.

"I know it's traditionally just you, me, Aunt Bess, and Jackie, but I feel really sorry for him with his wife out of town taking care of her sister."

"When is she supposed to be back?" Mom asked.

"I'm not sure."

"Well, it's all right with me if you invite him, and I'm sure Aunt Bess would be thrilled."

"I'll see what Jackie thinks," I said. "I do hate to break precedent."

"Well, as much as I enjoy our special Sunday lunches, we can't expect things to stay the same forever."

"I know." I blew out a breath. "I don't even know if Sheriff Billings can or will come, but I'd like to invite him if it's all right with Jackie."

After clearing it with Jackie, I called the police station.

"Billings," was the abrupt answer I received.

"Hi, Sheriff Billings. It's Amy Flowers."

"Everything all right?" he asked.

"Yes, sir. I didn't see you yesterday and wondered if Molly's back home yet."

"Not yet. But I knew how busy the Down South Café would be with the farmers' market going on, and I didn't want to get in the way. I just ate my sandwiches and chips yesterday."

"We were busier than we were last Saturday," I admitted. "I even had to throw together a batch of brownies and bake some cookies so that Oscar, Luis, and Scott would have some goodies to take home."

"Scott? Is he new?" the sheriff asked. "I remember Oscar from last week—he worked the cash register. Is Scott another of Luis's brothers?"

"No. He's a friend of HJ Ostermann." I didn't want to divulge the whole story of Scott's identity and connection to Gladys Pridemore, so I changed the subject. "I'm calling to invite you to lunch at the big house. If you're unable to leave your post, I'll be glad to bring a plate to you at the station."

"As long as I keep my phone and radio handy, there shouldn't be a problem with my leaving here for an hour or so. I'd be honored to have lunch with you ladies. Before I forget, though, how was dinner with Ryan and his parents?"

I hesitated.

"That bad, huh?" the sheriff teased.

"No. Not really. You were right about the dynamics, though. Ryan's father seemed to like me, and his mother definitely did not. She intimated that I needed to watch my weight, doesn't seem to care for my career choice, and asked if it bothered me that Ryan and Ivy had dated."

"She believes Ivy and Ryan were an item?" He hooted with laughter. "Ivy's husband won't be happy to hear about that."

"Ivy is married?" I asked.

"Yes, but you didn't hear that from me. Ivy Donaldson is the most private person I know, and she'd shoot me if she knew I divulged one of her secrets."

"So...we'll see you at the big house at noon?"

"I'll be there!"

I didn't realize what a monster I'd created until I got to the big house.

Mom met me at the door. "Hi, sweetheart. I didn't want Sheriff Billings to feel out of place being the only male here, so I've invited Clark."

"Oh...okay." I went into the kitchen where Jackie was paring apples as if she had a serious grudge against them. "What's wrong?"

She didn't look at me. "If I'd known we were going to completely break with tradition, I'd have invited Roger to join us today."

"Then call him," I urged. "And ask him to bring another dozen eggs while he's at it."

Aunt Bess had wandered into the kitchen and heard our conversation. She patted my shoulder. "No good deed goes unpunished. You'd better invite Ryan, or else he'll wonder why he was left out."

"You're right," I said.

"Of course, I am. I'm always right." She laughed as she trailed back into the living room.

When I called and invited Ryan to lunch, he said, "I thought Sunday lunch was reserved for you, Jackie, your mom, and Aunt Bess."

"Normally, it is. Today, we're making exceptions."

After talking with Ryan, I walked over and put my hand on Jackie's arm. "I'm sorry I turned today into a fiasco."

"You didn't...not really." Jackie smiled slightly. "We all knew our Sunday lunches would change one of these days."

"But you hate change," I said.

"True...but it's inevitable."

"Only for this week. Next week, everything will go back to normal."

Jackie merely smiled and preheated the oven for the rolls.

Chapter Thirteen

Aunt Bess insisted on sitting between Sheriff Billings and Clark Bennett at the dining room table. Almost immediately, she tried to get the lowdown on Gladys Pridemore's death.

"Do you believe Gladys was murdered, Sheriff?" she asked.

"Now, Bess, you know I can't tell you anything about an ongoing investigation."

"I'll take that as confirmation of the killing." Aunt Bess winked and nodded.

"Now, don't put words in my mouth," the sheriff said.

"Gladys Pridemore...I read her obituary in the newspaper," Clark said. "Professional curiosity, you know—I always need to check to see if any of my patients have died."

Mom laughed.

"But you're new here in Winter Garden," I said. "I hope your patients aren't dying off already."

"I hope so too." Clark chuckled. "Again, checking the obits is a habit. I've done it every morning for years."

"You're probably fine as long as you don't come across your own," Roger said, as he scooped hash brown casserole onto his plate.

"That's true." Clark turned to Sheriff Billings. "What was Ms. Pridemore's cause of death? The newspaper mentioned that she died after falling ill at her home, but what was the etiology?"

I saw Ryan and Sheriff Billings exchange glances.

"That's the part that's under investigation," Sheriff Billings said. "We aren't at liberty to discuss it."

"Ah, gotcha." Clark nodded. "It just piqued my interest—that's all."

"It makes me curious about the goings-on in Winter Garden myself," Aunt Bess said. "And I think it's a shame that people who are dining at my table won't even talk with me about a murder that practically took place in my own backyard."

"Don't worry—you're safe." Sheriff Billings reached for a ham roll. "And we'll talk about everything as soon as we're able to do so."

"What about the fire?" Aunt Bess asked. "Do you think it was set in order to destroy evidence? Because I do. I was there, you know."

"I am aware of that, and I'd appreciate it if you didn't put yourself in harm's way anymore." He bit into the roll.

"I didn't put myself in danger." Aunt Bess raised her chin. "I *am* the danger. I took pictures you might be able to use in your investigation. One of them shows a man—most likely the arsonist—fleeing the scene of the crime."

"Really?" Clark asked. "That's fascinating. I'd like to see those photos after lunch if you don't mind."

"I don't mind in the least."

As Aunt Bess looked like the cat—the *dangerous* cat—who swallowed the canary, I studied Clark Bennett from across the table. I got the feeling he was avoiding my eyes, and I wondered why he was so eager to see Aunt Bess's photographs. Was he nosy, patronizing, or downright guilty of something?

Gayle Leeson

Later that evening, Ryan and I were at my house watching a movie. While the movie was paused for drink and snack refills, I asked Ryan what he thought of Clark.

"I don't really know him," he said, returning the jug of sweet tea to the refrigerator. "I thought he seemed nice enough at lunch. What do you think of him?"

"I've got a bad feeling about him. I get the impression he's hiding something."

"Like what?"

"I don't know," I said. "You're the detective. That's why I want your take on the man."

"I don't have one. Do you truly believe Clark is hiding something, or would you simply rather the man date someone other than your mom?"

Pouring party mix into a smaller bowl, I said, "I don't have a problem with Clark Bennett dating my mother."

"Uh-huh."

I rolled my eyes at the unbridled skepticism I heard in his voice. "Fine. I *do* have a problem with it, but I wouldn't have any issues with the man whatsoever if I didn't suspect he's playing games with Mom."

"What kind of games?" Ryan asked.

"Well, he's still awfully friendly with Shelly."

"Have you shared your concerns about Clark with your mom?"

"No. I don't want to hurt her," I said.

"You know what hurts? What hurts is having a member of your family be dismissive of someone you're dating due to a silly misconception or misunderstanding."

Though Ryan had spoken softly, the words struck me hard. I hadn't considered how Ryan's mother's behavior had made him feel. I stepped over and hugged him. "I'm sorry."

"You don't owe me an apology," he said, as his arms came up and held me close.

"I'll talk with Mom later."

"Later is good." Ryan kissed me.

After Ryan left that evening, Rory and I walked up to the big house. It was still light enough that I didn't need a flashlight, but the frogs and crickets had come out to serenade us. Rory stopped to sniff at every fence post, marking his territory at various intervals.

When I neared the house, I saw a candle burning on the porch. I knew Mom must be outside because she always burned a citronella candle to keep the bugs away if she sat on the porch in the evening.

Rory ran on ahead and was standing on his hind legs with his front paws on Mom's lap when I reached the porch. Mom was scratching the terrier's head and telling him he was a good boy.

I took a seat on the white wooden rocker beside Mom's chair.

"I'm glad you're here," Mom said. "I missed talking with you today...you know, just us."

"I missed that too. And I'm sorry for the way I treated Clark. I didn't give him a very warm welcome, and that was wrong of me."

"You weren't *un*kind." Mom was quiet for a moment. Then she said, "I like him."

"I know. And that scares me because I don't want you to get hurt."

Jenna laughed. "Welcome to my world! Can you imagine how I felt when you left for college?"

"Not really."

She shook her head. "No. You can't. Not until you have children of your own. But, sweetheart, getting hurt is a possibility in any situation and in any relationship. You simply have to trust me to use my best judgment, just like I trust you to use yours."

"Speaking of *best judgment*, where's Aunt Bess?" I asked.

"She said she was going up to bed, but it's more likely she's trying to figure out how to get Sheriff Billings to deputize her."

I laughed. "Do you realize the fire crew is crazy about her?"

"Oh, yeah," Mom said. "They adore her. I think she might even be an honorary member of the crew."

"Just as long as they don't put her behind the wheel of a firetruck."

On Monday morning, I got a call at the café before we'd even officially opened. The call was from a tour director who'd be passing through Winter Garden with a church group in approximately two hours and would like to stop for breakfast at the Down South Café.

Dilly, Walter, and Jackie came through the door just in time to hear me say, "Our staff will be delighted to accommodate your group."

"What group?" Dilly asked.

Jackie groaned. "What's this about being delighted?"

"There's a church group coming through here from Roanoke," I explained. "They're going to be here in a couple of hours."

"We should call Donna in," Jackie said. "I'll need to help you with the cooking, and Shelly will need all the help she can get."

"True. I'll make the call." As I put on my headset to call Donna, I heard Dilly lamenting the fact that they were too hungry to wait for two hours until a church group showed up to eat.

"But I sure would like to know where they're going," she said.

"I'll let you know," Jackie promised.

I went into the kitchen and called Donna so I could start on my prep work while I talked. Donna told me she could work but that she could only be there during the time the church group would be there since she had a dental appointment at eleven. I told her that'd be fine and expressed my appreciation for her pitching in on such short notice.

As soon as I'd ended the call to Donna, I tore off a piece of bread from the end slice and put it between my lips before I began chopping onions so the onions wouldn't make my eyes tear. This was how Jackie found me when she came to deliver the bad news that Shelly was sick and wouldn't be in today.

"What?" The bread tumbled from my mouth onto the floor. "She *has* to work! What are we going to do?"

"Is Donna coming?"

"Yes, but only during the time the church group is here. She has a dental appointment." I picked up my bread and tossed it out the back door. "Did Shelly sound like she was truly sick?"

"I don't know." Jackie put her hands on her hips. "Do you want me to go over there and examine the woman myself?"

"No. I can't spare you." I took off my gloves and retrieved my phone from my purse beneath the counter. I scrolled through the contacts until I found Scott. "I'll call Scott and see if he can come in."

"Is Scott that sweet young man who was waiting tables on Saturday?" Dilly asked.

"He is." I called Scott and he agreed to come in as soon as he could get ready. I directed my attention back to Dilly and Walter. "Now that our crisis is averted, what would you like for breakfast?"

Dilly ordered French toast with a biscuit on the side for the raccoon, and Walter asked for pancakes with a side of oatmeal. Before I could head into the kitchen to get started, Dilly had more questions about Scott.

"How did you meet this fellow Scott?" she asked.

Since there were no other customers in the café at the time, I felt obliged to chat for a moment.

"He's a friend of HJ Ostermann, and he works at the Ostermann's corn maze." I frowned slightly. "From what I can gather, he hangs around there a lot."

"You talk like that's a bad thing," Walter said. "Why is that?"

"I don't necessarily think it's a bad thing. It's just that when the Pridemore basement caught on fire, Aunt Bess went out there and took some photographs and someone looking like Scott was captured in a couple of shots." I flipped my palms. "Don't get me wrong—Scott admitted he was there, and he told me he believed Malcolm Pridemore set the fire."

"But you don't sound convinced that you can trust the young man," Walter said, as he added sugar to the coffee Jackie had poured for him.

"Too bad Gladys isn't still alive," Dilly said. "She could've told you pert near anything you'd want to know about Scott, the Ostermanns, the mail carrier, the people visiting the corn maze." She chuckled.

"Ms. Pridemore was inquisitive then?" Jackie asked.

"Inquisitive?" Dilly laughed even harder at that. "Gladys Pridemore was as nosy as a four-year-old boy at his big sister's sleepover. Why, she even kept her husband's binoculars by the dining room window to make certain she never missed a trick."

"You think Gladys spied on the Ostermanns?" I asked.

"Honey, that woman spied on everybody...or, at least, everybody within binocular range."

I didn't know *how* Gladys Pridemore had been murdered, but Dilly might've provided one heck of a motive. Could Gladys have discovered someone's secret—a secret someone would kill to keep?

Both Donna and Scott arrived at the café about half an hour before the church group arrived. I was relieved to see them, and I imagine Jackie was too.

Just before the servers' arrival, a photography class from a nearby college had stopped in for coffee and baked goods. One of the students said they were going on a hike and would be taking photos of some of the local flora and fauna.

As the church bus pulled in, Jackie muttered to me, "It's unusual to be this busy on a Monday morning...and it's not even nine o'clock yet."

"What's the most unusual is that Shelly called in sick for the first time I can remember—today of all days." I shook my head and then greeted the group as they filed through the door.

When the dust settled and both the church group—who were on their way to West Jefferson, North Carolina to see the churches of the frescoes painted by the renowned artist Ben Long—and the students had gone to pursue their various adventures, Donna said, "Well, that was kinda fun." She looked at the rest of us. "Wasn't it?"

"I thought it was rad," Scott said. "I made a bunch of tips, and we sold a lot of merch."

"Merch?" I followed his gaze to the shelves behind the register. Our supply of *Down South Café* t-shirts and mugs had nearly been depleted.

"I'm sorry to run," Donna said. "I'd much rather stay here than go to the dentist...but to the dentist I must go."

"Relax and think happy thoughts," Scott told her.

"Thank you, Donna, for making yourself available on such short notice," I said. "You, too, Scott."

"I'm happy to help, and I'm even happier for the money," Scott said.

Homer arrived, and Scott greeted him with an enthusiastic, "Guru Guy! Whose wisdom are you sharing today?"

"Mr. Samuel Clemens, better known as Mark Twain," Homer said. "Did you know that Mr. Twain was born in November of 1835 soon after Halley's Comet made an appearance?"

"I did not." Scott's answer was so earnest that I had to suppress a giggle.

"The thing only comes around every seventy-five years or so, you know. Well, Mr. Twain is said to have told folks that he came in with that comet and would go out with it too."

Scott nodded. "That's awesome. Did he?"

"He died the day after the comet returned." Homer spread his hands. "At least, that's how I heard it."

Jackie and I were in the kitchen when Ryan came into the café. I heard Scott tell him, "Ryan, you're just in time."

I stiffened and scrunched up my face.

"Do you honestly think that if you close your eyes, he won't see you?" Jackie joked.

"It's not me I'm worried about him seeing."

"Yeah, well..." She jerked her head toward the dining room. "Go on. I'll man the grill."

I took a deep breath and opened the kitchen door. "Hey!" I forced all the sunshiny brightness I could muster into my voice.

"Hey yourself," Ryan said. "I hear I'm just in time."

"For what?" I asked.

"For Homer to share with us some words of wisdom from Mark Twain," Scott answered. "The floor is yours, Guru Guy."

Ryan arched a brow at me, and I shrugged.

Homer sipped his coffee and then cleared his throat. "'Whenever you find yourself on the side of the majority, it is time to pause and reflect.'"

"Whoa. That is deep." Scott grabbed a coffee pot and refilled Homer's cup.

"Amy, do you have a second?" Ryan asked.

"Sure." I moved closer to the counter.

"Outside?"

"Yeah...no problem." I smiled brightly as I strode toward the door. "Oh, hey, the sun is shining. We've barely had time to look out today."

When we stepped out the front door and it closed behind us, Ryan asked, "What's he doing here?"

"Who? Scott?"

"No. Homer—the one who comes in at the same time every day to order the same meal. *That's* the *him* I'm talking about."

"Now, there's no need for sarcasm. Shelly called in sick this morning right after I learned there was a church group planning to stop by. I'd already called Donna, and she came in for a little while but then she had to leave—dental appointment. Anyway, when I found out Shelly wouldn't be here, I asked Scott if he could come in." I looked up into Ryan's beautiful eyes. "I didn't know what else to do."

Ryan was frowning. "Shelly called in sick?"

I nodded. "It struck me as odd too. I don't think she's ever taken an unplanned day off, and then today of all days—"

His frown had deepened, and he was shaking his head.

"What?" I asked.

"I saw Shelly driving back into town from the direction of Abingdon about thirty minutes ago."

"Oh. That must be where her doctor's office is located." A tiny golden leaf floated down onto his shoulder, and I smiled as I brushed it away. "Now that things have slowed down, I should call her and see how she's feeling."

"I don't believe she'd been to the doctor's office," Ryan said. "It looked to me like she had her doctor—or, at least, *a* doctor—with her."

Chapter Fourteen

I stomped through the dining room on my way back to the kitchen. Homer tried to tell me some Mark Twain quote about anger, but I didn't listen.

"Would you mind going out there and taking Ryan's lunch order for the station?" I asked Jackie.

"Sure, but will you tell me what's got you so riled up first?"

"Shelly wasn't sick today. She was out galivanting with Clark Bennett." I picked up a spatula and flipped the burger Jackie had on the grill. "I'm going to see her after work, and she's going to explain why she lied to us this morning."

"I'll go with you," Jackie said. "Now, take a deep breath and blow out all those bad feelings. You've got to set them aside so you can work."

"Since when are you the calm, rational one?"

"Since you walked outside and left your sanity out there in the parking lot."

I blew out a breath. "You're right."

"Do you need a minute?"

"No." I waved her on. "I'm fine."

Together, we worked to get the orders ready so Ryan could get back to work. He told me he'd see me after work.

Then I apologized to Homer for my rudeness, and he wisely didn't try to repeat the anger quote. I went back to the kitchen, once again fuming to Jackie that Shelly had lied to us and that Clark Bennett was playing my mother for a fool.

"I'll hold down the fort if you want to leave right now and go confront Shelly," Jackie said.

"No. That would be unfair to you. Plus, I need to calm down so I can deal with Shelly rationally."

"Then you're going to have to set your feelings aside. The lunch rush is about to hit, and I need you to either help me or get out of my way."

"You're absolutely right," I admitted. "Would you mind doing most of the cooking for a little while? It might lift my mood to be around people. You know, if I have to pretend cheerfulness, maybe I'll start to feel it."

"Do what you need to do. After work, we'll go see Shelly together."

I took an order pad and pen and headed out to the dining room.

"You okay, Amy?" Luis asked as he was heading toward the kitchen with a bin filled with dirty dishes.

"I will be. I just need a break from the kitchen for a little bit." I smiled. "I thought it would do me good to mingle with the customers."

He shook his head. "Not me. When I'm in a bad mood, I want to get as far away from people as I can." He went on into the kitchen.

Scott sidled next to me. "I don't want to cloud your vibe or anything, but if things go south with Shelly, I'm available to work."

"Thanks. I appreciate that."

I spotted Malcolm Pridemore trudging toward the front door. I glanced over to gauge Scott's reaction. Would he confront Mr. Pridemore with his belief that Malcolm started the fire at the Pridemore house?

Scott started out from behind the counter, and I placed my hand on his arm.

"I'm good," he told me. "I won't embarrass you or disrespect your establishment. I promise." He strode across the dining room and opened the door. "Good afternoon, and welcome to the Down South Café."

Mr. Pridemore was leaning heavily on his cane today, and he sat at a table near the door. "Thank you, young man." He squinted at Scott. "I know you...don't I? Haven't I seen you with that Ostermann boy?"

"Yes, sir. Would you like to hear about our lunch special today?"

"No. I know what I want. I'd like a cheeseburger. The beef must be medium well with an internal temperature of 150 degrees—"

"I'm sorry, Mr. Pridemore," I interrupted, "but the minimum safe temperature for a burger is 160 degrees Fahrenheit."

"Is that a fact?" he asked, leaning his head back so he could look down his long nose at me.

"Yes. It's the USDA recommendation, and we strictly adhere to it."

Mr. Pridemore nodded once. "Very well." He then turned his attention back to Scott. "I'll have my burger cooked to the internal temperature of 160 degrees Fahrenheit—but not a degree more—with a single slice of Swiss cheese, three dill pickle slices, and one slice of tomato—yellow if you have it. I'd like potato salad for my side and lemonade to drink."

"Coming right up." Scott took the order to the window for Jackie.

"Mr. Pridemore, I'm sorry to hear there was a fire at your sister-in-law's house," I told him.

"I appreciate that. Nothing terribly valuable was lost...just a few things I'll now be saved the trouble of sorting through." He unwrapped his silverware from the napkin and examined the cutlery. I could tell he was making sure it was clean.

He continued speaking. "I hadn't realized my brother and his wife had accumulated such an eccentric load of junk. And, as executor of the estate, I have to go through all of it before I can dispose of the property. Very tedious business, I assure you."

Scott brought Mr. Pridemore his lemonade. "If there's anything else you need, please let me know. I'll have your food to you as soon as it comes up to the window."

Subdued, professional Scott was kinda sad...but I was glad he didn't start throwing around accusations in front of our customers.

Gayle Leeson

The lunch rush was winding down when Mom and Aunt Bess popped in for pie and coffee. Scott won Aunt Bess over immediately by greeting them with, "Good afternoon, beautiful ladies! How are you today?"

"I'm fine, sweetheart," she said. "How are you?"

"Better now that you're here. What can I get for you?"

I couldn't help but wonder if Aunt Bess recognized Scott from her photographs of the Pridemore house fire. But, of course, I hadn't been sure it was Scott in the pictures until he'd confessed to being there, and I was already acquainted with him. This was Aunt Bess's first introduction to Scott.

"We decided to come in for some pie," Mom said.

"Excellent choice." Scott moved over to the display case. "What flavor are you considering?"

"I'd like the Dutch apple," Mom said.

"And I want to see what looks good." Aunt Bess peered into the case. "That apple pie does look good...but then so does the chocolate coconut cream."

"Why don't you have a slice of each?" Scott asked her. "Life is short, and you could stand to put a little meat on your bones."

I walked over to stand beside Scott, who'd just persuaded my pleasantly plump great-aunt into having two slices of pie. Aunt Bess was smiling at him adoringly. If we weren't careful, she'd adopt the man and take him home with her. That's all Mom would need—an Aunt Bess *and* a Scott to babysit.

"Scott, this is my Aunt Bess—who is Jackie's grandmother, by the way—and my mom, Jenna," I said.

"Awesome to meet you," he said. "Now I see where Amy and Jackie get their good looks."

Aunt Bess reached up and patted her hair as if a single white curl would dare try to escape the rest of her shellacked helmet. "It's a pleasure to meet you, Scott. I'm going to take you up on your suggestion and have a small slice of each of those pies and a cup of French vanilla coffee please."

"Coming right up." Scott winked. "You'll have a scoop of vanilla ice cream with that pie, won't you?"

"Well, I will if you insist." Aunt Bess squeezed her shoulders forward and beamed like a schoolgirl.

"Jenna, would you like ice cream as well?" Scott asked.

"Please," Mom said.

"When you finish eating, I'd like to show you something I've got in my car, Mom," I said.

"Could you show me now while Scott is getting our pie ready?" she asked.

"Yeah...no problem." I came out from behind the counter and told Scott I'd be right back.

"Take as long as it takes," he said.

When I passed by Aunt Bess, she whispered not-so-quietly, "I like him better than Shelly."

I simply nodded.

Since we were pressed for time, I talked as we walked toward my car, which was at the far left side of the parking lot. I was taking Mom to see the insurance information I kept in my glove box. Of course, that wasn't the *real* reason we were going to my car. I had nothing whatsoever to show Mom, but that was our code when I wanted to speak with her privately. Mom has seen that proof-of-insurance information so often, the card is getting ratty.

"Jackie and I are—" I stopped, not wanting to tell Mom where my cousin and I planned to go after work. "—we have an errand to run this afternoon, and on the drive, I'm going to ask her to become a partner in Down South Café." I took a breath. "What do you think?"

"What do *you* think? Is this a spur of the moment idea, or have you given it careful thought?"

"I've been mulling the decision over for a while now," I said. "Jackie is my business partner in every other sense of the word. She's dedicated to the café, she's able to step in and manage the place for me if I'm sick or have to be away... I feel that offering her a partnership is the right thing to do."

Mom had a wide grin on her face when she hugged me. "I agree a hundred percent."

As we were strolling back toward the front door, we met Mr. and Mrs. Potts on their way out.

"Everything was lovely, dear," said Mrs. Potts, with a pat on my arm. "Have a good day now."

"You, too, and thank you."

As we walked back into the café, Aunt Bess was happily eating pie and regaling Scott with her adventure of taking Mom's SUV to the Pridemore house to "help investigate" the fire.

"You see, I realized right away that there was something fishy about that fire," she said. "I'm fairly certain it was arson."

"I totally agree," Scott said. "I was there that night too."

"You were?" Aunt Bess clapped her hands together. "You might be in some of my pictures."

"Show me." He got the apple pie back out of the display case while Aunt Bess was fishing her phone out of her large floral-print purse. "Let me get Jenna's pie and ice cream while you're finding your shots of the fire."

I was impressed with how well Scott plated the dessert. He even drizzled caramel onto the plate before he placed the pie and ice cream on it.

By the time Mom got her dessert, Aunt Bess had pulled up her photos from the night of the fire. "This could be you." She turned her phone toward Scott.

I saw that the image was the one that appeared to capture a man running away from the Pridemore house.

"Dude, that *is* me! I was trying to get out of there before the firefighters thought I was involved."

"Then you agree it was arson," Aunt Bess said.

"Oh, for sure," Scott agreed. "And I think that old dude Malcolm is the one who set the fire."

"You and I need to get together and compare notes." Aunt Bess dropped her phone into her purse. "I'm something of a Nancy Drew in Winter Garden."

"Don't you mean Jane Marple?" Mom asked wryly.

Aunt Bess gave her a scathing look. "Don't *you* mean you ought to shut up and eat your pie?"

Mom grinned at me and dug her spoon back into her pie.

"You're right," Scott said. "We *should* compare notes. Maybe together we can bring this guy down. Could we have coffee later?"

"We're going shopping after this, and I'm not sure what time we'll be back," Mom said quickly, after catching my look of alarm.

"Tomorrow works better for me anyhow," Scott said. "When and where would you like to meet?"

"My house...for lunch," Aunt Bess said.

Jackie came out of the kitchen. "I thought I heard your voice, Granny. What's going on?"

"Aunt Bess just invited Scott for lunch tomorrow," I said.

"And I'm accepting." He smiled at Aunt Bess. "It's a date."

"Jackie, maybe you could take them some food," I said.

"Yeah." She gave me a hard stare. "You'd better believe I will."

We had no time to discuss particulars because Phil Poston and his son ambled into the Down South Café with hot dogs and fries on their minds.

"I'm absolutely not all right with a suspected arsonist—and a possible murderer—being alone in the house with my grandmother and my aunt," Jackie ranted as she drove us to Shelly's house. "Are you? Are you okay with it?"

"Of course not. That's why I volunteered you to take them some food. And tonight, when Ryan gets to my house, I'm going to make him tell me if Scott is being seriously considered as a suspect in either the arson or in Gladys Pridemore's murder."

"Do you think he'll tell you?" she asked.

"Yes. Or, if nothing else, he'll tell me to get that lunch canceled if he believes Scott is a threat to Mom and Aunt Bess."

"I think we should cancel the lunch anyway." Jackie braked at a STOP sign and turned to look at me. "Whether he's a murderer or not, what do we really know about the guy?"

"Not much," I admitted. "But, hey, after we visit Shelly, I might be calling him to work tomorrow."

"Amy, I'm serious."

"So am I."

She pulled out into traffic, and we were both quiet. Not wanting to miss the opportunity to discuss the partnership with Jackie before we got to Shelly's house, I broke the silence.

"Would you like to become a partner in the Down South Café?"

"What brought that on?"

"You already do all the things a partner does," I said. "Why not make it official?"

"Wow. I'm...I'm floored." Her grip on the steering wheel tightened. "Do I have to give you an answer right now?"

"No. Take as much time as you need." I wanted to ask about her reservations, but I knew this was a decision Jackie needed to make for herself.

Chapter Fifteen

Shelly lived in a small, white house that was decorated pretty much like Jackie and I had expected: flower child bohemian meets shabby chic. Everything was pink, white, floral or lace. It actually suited Shelly, and I told her how pretty it was as we all took a seat in her living room. Much of my anger had evaporated, especially now that I saw Shelly—she really did look ill.

"Aw, I appreciate that, Amy, but it's a mess right now." Shelly tidied the fan of fashion magazines on her coffee table.

I didn't see a thing out of place in the tidy home and couldn't help but compare it to Nadine Ostermann's kitchen where I'd had to clean off a chair in order to sit down.

"Gee, I think it looks great," Jackie said. "When I'm sick, my apartment looks like a pig sty."

"We were going to bring you some food," I said, "but we were afraid to without knowing what's wrong. We came to see how you are, not make matters worse."

"Right." Jackie leaned forward. "So, what's wrong—stomach bug, cold, sore throat, migraine?"

"None of that." Shelly looked down at her clasped hands. "The truth is I'm not sick... unless you count heartsick. But this morning, it was simpler to say I was sick than to get into a long, drawn-out explanation. I'm sorry I lied."

"It's okay," I said. "Tell us what's going on."

"It's my mother." Shelly twisted her hands in her lap. "A while back, I started to notice some changes in her. Her hands were trembly, she was tired all the time, and she was starting to shuffle when she walked." She looked up at the ceiling for a moment to try to stem her tears. "When I asked her about it, she told me that was all part of getting old. But I knew better. When I hit forty, I started reading everything I could get my hands on about aging and slowing down the process."

"Granny is older than your mom, and she doesn't have any of those symptoms," Jackie said.

Shelly nodded. "I called Dr. Bennett's office last night expecting to get an answering machine or something, but he answered. We talked, and he told me it sounded like Parkinson's and that he'd refer Mama to a neurologist. Later on, he called me back and told me he'd arranged for his friend—a neurologist in Abingdon—to see her at ten-thirty this morning."

"Did the neurologist confirm Dr. Bennett's suspicions?" I asked.

Shelly's face crumbled, and she put her hand over her mouth.

I got out of my chair and hugged her. "I'm so sorry. How can I help?"

When she was composed enough to speak, Shelly said, "I'm moving Mama in with me. She's stubborn, but she knows she might need help from time to time."

"Isn't there some medication she can take? Something that will help?" Jackie asked.

"There is. Since his practice isn't officially open yet, Dr. Bennett went with Mama and me to the neurology appointment," Shelly said. "I was awfully glad he did. Between my being upset and listening to words I'd never heard before in my life, I was kinda shell-shocked when we left the neurologist's office. Dr. Bennett accompanied us back to Mama's house and explained everything to us in layman's terms."

"What's the prognosis?" I asked.

"It's a progressive condition, so there's no cure. While many people with Parkinson's are able to continue to live independently, I think it would be best—given her age—for Mama to move in here with me." Shelly wiped her eyes. "It's as much for me as it is for her. I told her I couldn't see a minute's peace if I had to wonder all the time if she'd fallen or something."

"I understand completely." I patted Shelly's shoulder. "That's why Mom moved into the big house with Aunt Bess after Nana died."

"The doctor gave Mama some medication, and she has an appointment with a physiotherapist day after tomorrow. Dr. Bennett was awfully good to pull strings on Mama's behalf."

"It sounds like you could use a few days off to take care of your mom," I told her.

"I hate to ask—" Shelly began.

"I insist." I glanced at Jackie. "We'll manage just fine for a few days."

"I know Donna will help out when she can, but what about Saturday and the farmers' market?" Shelly asked. "I have to be there then."

"Let's worry about Saturday closer to Saturday. Right now, your priority is getting your mother settled in." I gave her another hug. "Please let us know if there's anything we can do to help out."

"I will," Shelly promised.

When we got back into the car, Jackie squinted toward Shelly's porch.

"What is it?" I asked, looking at the porch to see what Jackie might be staring at.

"Aw, nothing. I just thought a glob of your self-reproach got caught on one of Shelly's macramé plant hangers when we walked by it."

I gave her the old side-eye glare. "Just drive."

That evening when Ryan arrived, his eyes widened when he saw the table. We were having filet mignon, loaded baked potatoes, grilled corn on the cob, rolls, banana pudding, and chocolate peanut butter cupcakes.

"I haven't done anything to deserve a meal like this," he said. "What's up?"

I kissed his cheek. "Just sit down and enjoy it while it's still hot."

"I can't enjoy it if I'm wondering what's going on with you the whole time I'm eating."

"You act like I never make you a nice meal," I said.

"Every meal you make for me is delicious, but this one is special. Even you have to admit that."

"Sit down and eat." I pulled out his chair. "Please. We can talk while we eat."

"Ah-ha. That's it. Here we go." Ryan sat down. "This meal is a bribe, isn't it?"

"Don't look at it that way." I sat across from him. "I just need to know how you feel about Scott...not necessarily as a person, but as a suspect."

"You know—"

"Yes, I know you can't discuss an ongoing investigation. But, if you were me, would you feel comfortable having Scott in the house alone with Mom and Aunt Bess?"

"No," Ryan said, cutting into his steak. "But what reason would he have for being in the house alone with Jenna and Bess?"

I explained that earlier today Scott and Aunt Bess had been discussing the Pridemore house fire while Mom and Aunt Bess were at the café. "Aunt Bess decided that she and Scott needed to compare notes and solve the crime, so she invited Scott to the big house for lunch tomorrow."

He stilled. "That's not a good idea."

"Jackie and I didn't think so either, and since Shelly is going to be off work for a few more days and Scott has agreed to work in her place, the problem is solved for now," I said. "But Aunt Bess won't let this go."

Ryan rubbed his hand over his face. "Let me get this straight. You're not comfortable with Scott having lunch with your mom and Aunt Bess, but you trust him to work in Shelly's place at the café?"

"Well, sure. That's entirely different."

"How? You don't want a murder suspect in close proximity to people you care about," he said. "Well, guess what? Neither do I."

"Scott is a suspect in Gladys Pridemore's murder?" I asked. "I knew he was under suspicion of setting the fire but not of murder. What motive could he possibly have for wanting to kill Gladys?"

"Suffice it to say, he's one of several suspects we're currently investigating." He took a bite of steak. "This is good. Thank you."

"You're welcome." I buttered a roll. "Could you tell me one thing? How exactly was Gladys Pridemore killed? Ivy initially thought there might be a gas leak or something, but, specifically, what killed the woman?"

"The autopsy findings suggested carbon dioxide poisoning."

My mind began whirring. Carbon dioxide. Plastic sealing the windows. The pot on the stove. "Dry ice."

"What?" Ryan asked.

"Dry ice. That's how Ms. Pridemore was killed."

"We came to that same conclusion, but we don't know how the killer got the dry ice into the room."

"I do," I said. "I believe the person who killed Ms. Pridemore started by putting a sedative of some kind in her coffee. Then when she passed out, the murderer put a substantial block of dry ice in that Dutch oven I found on the stove. The burner was on warm, so the ice probably melted more slowly."

"And since the room was sealed, the fumes suffocated her." Ryan stood. "I have to call the sheriff."

"Amy Flowers, I'm gonna end up having to deputize you yet," Sheriff Billings said, as he strode into my kitchen.

"Have a seat...and a cupcake," I said.

"Don't mind if I do." The sheriff took a cupcake with one hand and pulled out a chair with the other.

I poured Sheriff Billings a glass of iced tea before I sat down. I felt glad that Ryan and I had been able to finish dinner and get the kitchen cleaned up before Sheriff Billings arrived. Ryan seemed nervous. I knew he didn't want the sheriff to think he'd been doling out confidential information.

"Over dinner tonight, I asked Ryan if he thought it would be all right for Scott—one of the corn maze actors and a part-time server at the Down South Café—to spend time alone with my mom and Aunt Bess." I gave a little laugh. "It appears that Aunt Bess and Scott believe that if they put their heads together, they can prove that Malcolm Pridemore set the fire in Gladys Pridemore's basement."

Sheriff Billings licked frosting off his fingers. "Well, in the first place, I don't think your Aunt Bess needs any encouragement with her so-called investigating."

"Neither do I." I handed him a napkin. "And Ryan said that it wasn't a good idea to have Scott visiting her at home. But I've solved that problem for now—he'll be working for me tomorrow."

The sheriff leveled his gaze at Ryan.

Ryan nodded. "See what I'm dealing with here? She doesn't want a suspicious character alone with her mom and aunt, but she'll pay him to be at the café."

"How did you get onto the subject of how Gladys Pridemore died?" Sheriff Billings asked.

"When Ivy and I went back to the crime scene so I could walk her through what happened, she seemed convinced that a gas or airborne toxin was responsible for Ms. Pridemore's death," I said. "This, even though the spilled coffee would lead a person to surmise that the woman had drunk poison."

"Right." Sheriff Billings wiped his hands and mouth on a napkin. "I called Ivy before I came over and asked her if she could meet me here. She said she was in the middle of something and that I could fill her in tomorrow. Amy, she said if she has any questions for you, she'll stop by the café."

"Okay." I noticed that the sheriff's tea glass was getting low, so I got up and retrieved the pitcher from the refrigerator. "Ryan didn't speak out of turn. I want you to know that. He flat-out refuses to discuss cases with me."

"I know." Sheriff Billings thanked me for the refill and took a long drink. "But sometimes we can't help but let things slip to our loved ones; and in this instance, it's good he did. You might've put an important piece of the puzzle in place for us."

I looked at Ryan. I was still anxious to assure Sheriff Billings that Ryan hadn't given me any sensitive information about Gladys Pridemore's death...or, at least, nothing I hadn't already guessed. Ryan shook his head slightly to encourage me to let it go.

Sheriff Billings took a notebook from his shirt pocket and flipped through the pages. "On the day you and Jackie found Gladys Pridemore unresponsive at her kitchen table, you mentioned that you removed a pot from a burner and turned off the stove."

"That's right. It struck me as odd because during the call Ms. Pridemore—or the person claiming to be Ms. Pridemore—said she was ordering food because she didn't cook anymore. Then I entered the kitchen and found a pot on the burner."

"What size was the pot?" he asked.

"It was a ten-quart Dutch oven, so that's a substantial pot." I got up and took a similar pot from the cabinet. "This is a six-quart Dutch oven."

"So, the one at the Pridemore house was considerably bigger than that one," Ryan said.

"Right. My theory is that Gladys Pridemore was administered some sort of sedative in her coffee," I said. "Then her killer filled the Dutch oven with dry ice and turned the burner on low. Since the kitchen window had already been winterized, Jackie and I couldn't even get it open to air out the room when we arrived."

"Well, you're right about the coffee—there were traces of sleeping pills in it." Sheriff Billings raised his eyes from his notebook to pierce me with a stare. "You didn't hear that."

"No, sir, I did not."

"There was weather stripping on the kitchen door leading to the outside and on the interior kitchen door," Sheriff Billings continued. "That room was sealed as tight as Dick's hatband."

"And then somebody—most likely, the killer—called the Down South Café to ensure that Ms. Pridemore would be found," Ryan said.

"Do you think the killer intended to scare Ms. Pridemore rather than kill her?" I asked. "I mean, if we'd been there just a little bit sooner, Ms. Pridemore might still be alive."

"I seriously doubt that." The sheriff patted my hand. "Don't blame yourself, Amy. Too much damage had already been done to save Gladys Pridemore. And don't fool yourself either. The person who poisoned the air in that kitchen is a cold-blooded killer."

Chapter Sixteen

Donna wasn't able to work on Tuesday because she was still recovering from her dental procedure. Jackie and I explained to Luis and Scott that Shelly's mother was experiencing some health problems and that Shelly wouldn't be in for a few days.

"I'll be happy to fill in for Shelly for as long as you need me," Scott said. "I enjoy the work, and I need the money."

"Thank you, Scott."

Walter came in then, humming Beethoven's *Ode to Joy*. He swept out his arms before asking the question to which he already knew the answer. "Am I the first customer to arrive this morning?"

"Indeed, you are," I said.

"Young man," Walter said to Scott, "would you be so kind as to set me up with a cup of coffee while I await my lady friend?"

"Be happy to," Scott said.

While Scott was getting the coffee, Ivy strode into the café.

"Good morning, all," she said.

"Ivy, hi." I started out from behind the counter.

"Oh." Ivy's eyes widened. "Darn. I...I just remember there's somewhere else I have to be right now." With that, she rushed out the door.

I turned and looked at Scott.

He shrugged and served Walter's coffee. "Be right back to take your order."

"Take your time," Walter said.

I noticed that Scott was taking his phone out of his pocket as he stepped out onto the patio. I went into the kitchen, put on my headset, and called Ivy. The call went straight to voice mail. Had Ivy left because Scott was here? And, if so, could she be the person Scott had gone outside to call?

That's ridiculous. How could Ivy and Scott possibly know each other?

I went back out into the dining room after leaving Ivy a message. When Scott came back inside, he ducked his head and got the coffee pot in order to top off Walter's cup.

Dilly arrived as he was pouring the beverage and asked him to fill a cup for her as well. That seemed to be all it took to right Scott's course, and he went back to normal. Or, had he been normal all along, and was I merely scrutinizing him for abnormal behavior?

I greeted Dilly and then went back into the kitchen for breakfast preparations.

Ivy called me a couple of hours later as I was scrambling eggs. Thank goodness for headsets.

"I'm sorry you had to run off without even having coffee earlier," I said.

"Yeah...um...I'm usually not so scatterbrained. I'm having an off day."

I barked out a laugh. "For a second, I thought Scott scared you off."

"Oh. No." Ivy's words were clipped and rushed. "I spoke with Sheriff Billings last night, and he told me your theory about how Gladys Pridemore was murdered. Excellent deduction. The dissolving of dry ice on the stove would explain the odor you experienced as well as the headache and dizziness."

"Right," I said. "I can tell you're in a hurry, but I'm kinda concerned. Almost everyone with a motive to harm Gladys Pridemore was at the farmers' market on that Saturday."

"Yes, but I wouldn't worry about that, Amy. The vendors at the farmers' market have nothing against you, they're only there to make money, and there are a lot of people around. You'll be safe."

"Okay." I drew out the word, confused by Ivy's patronizing tone. "I didn't think our lives were in danger here at the café. I'm merely uneasy that Gladys Pridemore's killer hasn't been caught yet."

"I know." Her voice softened. "We're doing everything we can."

Homer's hero on Tuesday was the Scottish comedian Billy Connolly. It was apparent he was keeping things light—even to the point of affecting a terrible accent—when he quoted: "I've always wanted to go to Switzerland to see what the army does with those wee red knives."

I laughed harder than I normally would have because I still felt guilty about ignoring his anger quote when I'd been furious with Shelly yesterday. I still felt guilty about my anger toward Shelly too.

HJ Ostermann hurried into the café, ignored my greeting, and stood by the door to the patio waiting for Scott to finish taking the orders of Mr. and Mrs. Martin.

HJ looked rough. His sweatshirt and jeans looked as if they'd been slept in, and his hair was sticking up all over his head.

Scott glanced at HJ, and HJ jabbed his thumb in the direction of the patio.

For the second time today—or, actually, anytime—I saw Scott looking uncomfortable. He brought the Martins' order to the window, handed it to me, and then moved quickly back into the dining room. I peeped out the window to see if Scott was going out on the patio to meet with HJ. He was.

The two were standing in such a way that I could see them both from the side. HJ handed an envelope to Scott, and Scott shoved it into his back pocket. As Scott returned to the dining room, he said something to HJ. I couldn't hear what he'd said over the din.

I quickly hurried back to the grill and started preparing Mrs. Martin's French toast and Mr. Martin's Spanish omelet. They had an international theme going this morning, and I wondered if it had been deliberate. They could be a quirky little couple.

Jackie bounded through the kitchen door, and I gave a squeak of surprise.

"Was that the sound of your nosy conscience?" she asked.

"Don't go there. Not today. I know things today that I didn't yesterday, and I'd appreciate a little leeway."

"Fine." Jackie lowered her voice to the point that I had to put my head right next to hers to hear her. "Since you were so interested in Scott's interaction with HJ, I thought you might want to know that when Scott came in from the patio, he said, 'I'll take care of it.'"

"Take care of what?" I asked.

"I have no idea. Now...what's the new info?"

"I can't talk about it here. We'll discuss it after work when it's just the two of us."

Jackie opened her mouth to respond, but Luis came into the kitchen.

"What was that about Aunt Bess?" I asked her.

"Oh...yeah...I keep telling Granny to stay off the dating boards, but every time they have a free week-end, there she goes."

"I know," I said. "Aunt Bess is going to be the death of all of us."

Even though that wasn't our actual topic of conversation, I imagined truer words were never spoken.

That afternoon, Jackie and I decided to follow Scott to see if we could find out what he was taking care of for HJ. Since he was familiar with my yellow Bug and probably would recognize Jackie's car as well, Jackie had Roger bring his truck to the Down South Café parking lot prior to closing. Roger then came around to the back door where he and Jackie swapped keys.

After work, Jackie drove Roger's pickup truck, and we tailed Scott. In the movies and on television, when detectives were following a suspect through traffic, the cops could remain inconspicuous by keeping one or two vehicles between their car and the suspect. In Winter Garden, Virginia, where you and your suspect were in the only two automobiles on a rural road, it was a smidgeon more difficult to pretend you merely happened to be going in the same direction.

In fact, despite our being in Roger's truck, Scott peered into his rearview mirror and waved. Jackie and I waved back. What else could we do?

We tailed Scott to the interstate ramp heading south toward Bristol.

"Where's he going?" I asked Jackie.

"I have no idea, but wherever it is, you'd better be thinking up a good reason for us to be there too."

By the time Scott got off the interstate, there were a couple of vehicles between us. Not that it mattered—our cover was already blown.

We followed him to a Halloween specialty store. After he parked, he stood by his car and waited for us to find a space. Jackie pulled into a space in a deserted area of the lot since she wasn't accustomed to driving Roger's truck.

Scott met us halfway. "Hey! What're you guys doing here?"

"I'm hoping to find some Halloween decorations for the café," I said. "What about you? Replacing the werewolf costume?"

"No, I'm replacing the animatronic spider HJ broke...hopefully, before Harry finds out about it." Scott led the way to the Halloween shop's door. "Harry would be livid if he knew. He thinks HJ is irresponsible already."

"Why's that?" Jackie asked.

"Because after his divorce, HJ had to move back in with his parents," Scott said. "But, dudes, I get that—the job market is fierce. And I didn't know HJ before I moved to Winter Garden, but I'm catching a vibe that his parents blame him for the divorce."

"I'm a firm believer that there are always two sides to every story," I said.

Scott waffled his hand. "Not always...but usually." He held the door for Jackie and me to enter the shop ahead of him.

"Let me know if y'all need any help finding any-thing," a teenaged girl greeted us.

"No, no, no." Her manager stepped out from be-hind a curtain that hid a storage area. "Like this, Amber." The thin, abnormally pale—or wearing white makeup—man in the black cape stepped to the front of the counter. "Good eeeevening."

Scott nodded. "How you doing, Drac Dude?"

The manager ignored Scott's question and in-structed Amber, "Now, you try it."

She rolled her eyes. "Gewd eeevening."

"Awesome." Scott laughed and high-fived the girl while Jackie and I slipped away.

Most of the bigger merchandise was displayed in the open warehouse, which had wide aisles displaying costumes and smaller props. An Edwardian butler caught my eye, and I wandered over to him.

When I was close enough, the animatronic butler's eyes moved from side to side, and he said, "Welcome! Won't you stay for dinner?"

"That thing is creepy as all get out," Jackie said.

"Aw, come on," I said. "I kinda like him."

"May I take your head? I mean...*hat*...of course," the creepy butler said.

"Oh, man! Kids would love this guy," Scott said.

"No, they wouldn't. They'd hate him." Jackie shuddered. "*I* hate him."

I glanced at the price tag. "Yikes. I hate the price. Sorry, Jeeves, you won't be coming back to the Down South Café with us."

"Have a seat and let me *poison* you a drink." The doll's eyes shifted back and forth as it gave a guttural cackle.

"You two can stay here with lunatic Lurch if you want to," Jackie said. "I'm going to look for something I *don't* want to smash with a bat."

"I think she might actually do it," Scott said quietly.

"Yeah...I'm pretty sure she would." I smiled. "It's a good thing I can't afford him. I had no idea these props were so expensive."

"Oh, for real. The spider I have to get is nowhere near as pricey as this guy, but it's still over a hundred bucks." He patted the envelope in the back pocket of his jeans. "HJ gave me a hundred and fifty, and that'll be cutting it close."

I walked over to where Jackie was looking at superheroine costumes while Scott went to buy a giant jumping spider from either Amber or her manager.

"These costumes bring back so many memories," I said, placing my hand on her shoulder.

"Doesn't it though?" She smiled. "Who could forget that year I dressed up as Batgirl, you were Wonder Woman, Roger was Superman, and Sarah was Cat Woman?"

"Or the time we trick-or-treated as the Power Rangers?"

Jackie laughed and began singing the show's theme song.

"I *loved* that show," Scott said, as he walked toward us. "Are you talking about costumes you wore as kids?"

"Yeah," I said. "Tell us one of your favorites."

"The only time my sister and I coordinated our costumes was when she dressed up as Daphne from *Scooby Doo*." He grinned. "I was Shaggy. Come to think of it, those characters still suit us."

After leaving the Halloween shop, Jackie called Roger, and I called Ryan and arranged to meet for dinner at an Italian restaurant in Abingdon. We asked Ryan to pick up Roger so that we'd have only two vehicles at the restaurant. If Ryan wondered why Jackie and I were tooling around in Roger's pickup truck, he didn't ask. And I thought it best to wait until we were at the restaurant to volunteer any information.

Jackie and I were the first to arrive. We got a table and ordered soft drinks.

"What's your opinion of Scott?" I asked Jackie after the waitress had left to get our drinks.

"I'd like him fine if he wasn't suspected of arson and murder."

"Do you really think he's capable of either of those things?" In my mind, I couldn't imagine Scott doing either, but I'd been wrong about people before.

"I'd hate to think so," Jackie said, but who knows?"

"Too bad we can't ask Gladys Pridemore," I murmured.

"If we could ask her, we wouldn't be having this conversation."

"I know. I just meant that she was apparently looking through those binoculars all the time. Who knows what secrets she could tell?"

Jackie said, "Too bad she didn't take photographs."

"Wait...what if she did?"

Before Jackie could answer, the server brought our drinks. Roger and Ryan arrived, and Jackie waved them over.

"What have you two been up to?" Ryan asked, sliding into the booth next to me. "Roger told me that all he knew was that you were on a top-secret surveillance mission."

"Some detectives we turned out to be," Jackie said. "The person we were surveilling waited for us in the parking lot and then held the door open and ushered us into his destination."

Roger laughed. "And what *was* his destination?"

"The Halloween specialty store," I said. "I got a few decorations for the café, so Jackie and I had a perfectly logical reason for being there...in your truck."

"You bought a truckload of decorations?" Ryan asked.

"Not quite," I said.

"Had she got the creepy butler she wanted, he'd have ridden shotgun, and you'd have had to come to Bristol and pick me up," Jackie told Roger. "And you would have had to give me a job on your construction crew."

"Hold up." Ryan waved his hands. "I can't imagine your being afraid of a mechanical doll."

Jackie lifted her chin. "I am not *afraid* of them. I just despise them. Ever since these two made me watch that stupid evil red-haired killer doll when we were kids, I've hated talking dolls."

"We didn't *make* you," I protested.

"Nope." Roger grinned. "But I did double dog dare you."

We had so much fun at dinner that it completely slipped my mind to ask Ryan if the forensic team had recovered a cell phone or camera at Gladys Pridemore's house. My question about whether or not Ms. Pridemore had a penchant for photography would be answered soon enough anyway.

Chapter Seventeen

At about half-past nine o'clock on Wednesday morning, Malcolm Pridemore came into the café. He looked around the dining room.

"That unpleasant little man who was rude the first day I patronized your establishment isn't here, is he?"

I hid a smile as I recalled that Homer was "rude" to Mr. Pridemore because Mr. Pridemore had been rude to us. "No, sir. He won't be in for another hour or so."

"Good." Mr. Pridemore sniffed. "Normally, I could tolerate his drivel well enough, but today I have a headache."

I noticed the man did look a tad pale. "I'm sorry to hear that. Maybe some coffee will help."

"I do hope so, Ms. Flowers. I spent most of yesterday going through one solitary room—the dining room—sorting Gladys' things. You can't imagine the sheer tediousness of that task."

"No, I can't." I poured Mr. Pridemore's coffee. "I certainly don't envy you."

"I brought a box of cookbooks that were at the bottom of the china cabinet. I thought you might like to put them to good use."

"How considerate." I raised my hand to my throat. "Thank you."

"You'd like them then?" he asked.

At my nod, he looked around the dining room until he spotted Luis and Scott clearing off some tables. "Perhaps one of these strong young men would carry the box in from the passenger side of my car? It's the black sedan parked in the handicapped space."

"I'll do it," Scott said.

"I appreciate that." Mr. Pridemore used his key fob to unlock the car.

"I'm not surprised Ms. Pridemore had so many cookbooks," I said, "given her allergy and everything."

"Her allergy?" he asked.

"Yes. The potato allergy."

He raised his bushy eyebrows. "You know, I'd forgotten all about that. Our families didn't dine together often."

Scott brought the box inside and placed it on the counter beside the register. I went over to get a closer look at its contents. I certainly didn't need more cookbooks, but I couldn't resist them. Besides, I'd never been one to look a gift horse in the mouth.

"May I take your order, Mr. Pridemore?" Jackie asked. "With Amy having her head in those books, who knows how long it'll be before she comes up for air."

Mr. Pridemore ordered in his usual persnickety way. I wasn't even paying attention.

"These look fantastic," I said, as I lifted each book out of the box and gave it a cursory examination. There was a cookbook by Dorie Greenspan, one by Julia Child, a vegetarian cookbook...this box truly was a find.

Mr. Pridemore tasted his coffee. "And I believe you'll agree they're a bargain at only thirty dollars for the lot."

"What was that?" I asked.

Jackie snorted and had to rush into the kitchen to cover her laughter. Luis's back was turned, but I could see his shoulders shaking. I was willing to give the man thirty dollars for the books...and I wanted to cover my embarrassment in thinking Mr. Pridemore was gifting me the books. After all, he was correct that they were well worth that amount.

Scott had other ideas. He decided to negotiate. "Amy will give you fifteen for the entire box, or she can go through and pick which ones she wants. You can give her the individual prices of the books she chooses, and you can take the others back with you."

"No, indeed. I'll not take any detritus back into that house," Malcolm Pridemore said. "Fifteen dollars *plus* twenty percent off my meal."

"It's a deal," I said quickly.

As soon as Malcolm Pridemore left the café, Scott pulled me aside. "I'm sorry I overstepped about the books, but that old dude ticks me off. Guess what I saw in his car?"

"What?" In my imagination, it could be anything from a severed head to a bright pink tutu...though I'd have been more shocked to learn that it was a tutu. A tutu would likely mean that Mr. Pridemore had a granddaughter, and I had a tough time imagining Mr. Pridemore as a doting grandpa. Did the fact that I could more easily imagine Mr. Pridemore as a murderer say more about him or about me?

"A bunch of expensive stuff," Scott said. "There was a sterling silver tea set—the real thing because it needed to be polished, a camera, figurines, dishes..."

"Maybe he's having to sell some things to pay off the estate's debts," I said. "Or maybe she left those things to him in her will." My brain caught up to the items Scott had mentioned. "Did you say he had a camera?"

He nodded.

"What kind of camera?" I asked.

"It looked like one of those that spits out the picture as soon as you take it and then develops right in front of you," he said.

"That's weird."

"Dude...right?" He crossed his arms. "We need to let somebody know Malcolm Pridemore is making off with all that stuff."

"I'll talk to Ryan about it," I said. "Thanks."

Scott saw that Homer was walking toward the door, so he uncrossed his arms and hurried over to open the door. "Hi, Guru Guy. We're glad to see your friendly face."

"I appreciate that," Homer said. "Like the author Robert Louis Stevenson, I believe a man is successful if he has lived well, laughed often, and loved much."

"Well, some people enjoy going around like an old grump," Scott said.

"Good morning, Homer." I brought him a cup of coffee. "I'll get started on your sausage biscuit."

"Thank you." Homer turned back to Scott. "Mr. Stevenson also said, 'Everybody, soon or late, sits down to a banquet of consequences.' Which means we all sometimes have to eat a little crow." He chuckled. "I added that last bit myself."

I was relieved to get home on Wednesday afternoon. It had seemed like an extra long day. After I fed the pets, I soaked in a warm Epsom salt bath. When I got out of the tub, I put on white satin pajamas. I didn't care that it was not even six o'clock yet. I had no intention of leaving the house again until morning.

I ate an egg salad sandwich and then pulled the box of Gladys Pridemore's cookbooks over to the sofa. Princess Eloise had taken up residence on the windowsill, and Rory was playing in the backyard. It was a peaceful evening.

The first cookbook I plucked from the box was filled with delicious sounding French recipes: Croque monsieur, chicken Provençal, steak au poivre, coq au vin. I recalled Mom telling me once that coq au vin must've been the ultimate sophisticated dish to 1960s television writers because it was served on episodes of both *Bewitched* and *The Dick Van Dyke Show*. I wasn't sure the Down South Café patrons were ready for coq-au-vin-level elegance, so I put the French cookbook aside for the time being.

The second book on the stack was titled *Recipe for a Cooked Goose Plus Other Dishes for Life*. The image on the front cover was that of a cartoon goose with black Xs for eyes. I thought that was a terribly unappetizing graphic to put on a cookbook.

But when I opened the book, I realized that it wasn't a cookbook at all. The *recipes* were actually verses or compositions for living. There was a section called *For A Happy Family* and included a recipe for a happy home. The recipe called for cups of love, kindness, laughter, and forgiveness.

It was in the *Recipes for Disaster* section that I found the titular dish.

Cooked Goose
Ingredients:

1 cup boredom
2 cups temptation
1 heaping tablespoon delusion
A liberal dash of arrogance
Serve with indiscretion. Voila! Your goose is cooked!

I smiled and thought Mom and Aunt Bess would get a kick out of this book. I closed the thin volume and was placing it onto the end table when something nearly fell out from between the pages. The corner of the object made me think it might be an index card, but when I pulled it out, I could see that it was a photo.

The picture had been taken from some distance away, but I could tell that the man in the photograph was HJ Ostermann. He was laughing with a woman. Although they had their heads close together, I could see that he was with Fran, the woman he'd brought into the café on the day I'd met Scott. Fran's hair was longer in the photo, and the image appeared to have been captured in the early spring. Had HJ been involved with Fran while he was still married? Could that be why his parents blamed him for the divorce?

I held the book upside down and flipped the pages. More photographs fell onto my lap. I'd been right about Ms. Pridemore having a camera. Of course, Scott had been right too—while the instant camera Ms. Pridemore had used had a zoom lens, the quality wasn't the best. Still, I could imagine they served their purpose.

I examined each of the pictures. In one, Harry appeared to be hiding something under a rock outside the barn. There was a photo of a field—just an empty, weedy lot. The image was slightly blurred, and I wondered why Ms. Pridemore had even kept it. Maybe she thought it proved that the Ostermanns weren't properly caring for the property. After all, Sarah said Ms. Pridemore had been hoping to break the lease-to-own agreement. The final photo was of Nadine and Scott embracing. My heart sank. Proof of an affair was certainly a motive for murder.

The next morning, Sheriff Billings came in for breakfast.

"Molly still not back from her sister's house yet?" Jackie asked.

Gayle Leeson

"Not yet," he said. "But her sister has a doctor's appointment today. I'm hoping it'll be good news and that Molly will be heading back home this weekend."

"I hope so too." I filled his coffee cup, and then lowered my voice. "I have something to bring you after work."

"Good. What *is* the special of the day?"

"It's meatloaf, but that's not what I'm talking about." I looked around to make sure everyone was busy and that no one—especially Scott—was listening. "I might have new evidence in the Gladys Pridemore case." I raised my voice back to a normal volume. "Besides you and Ryan, is there anyone else working this evening?"

"Our dispatcher will be there."

I smiled. "I'll bring enough for everybody."

After that, I went back into the kitchen and didn't come out until Homer arrived.

"Man, I hope you can cheer Amy up today," Scott said to Homer as soon as the man walked through the door. "She's been in Dumpsville all morning."

I had *not* been in Dumpsville, but I was admittedly quieter and more reserved than usual. Jackie had also noticed and had asked me in the kitchen if I was feeling all right. I'd told her I was fine and that we'd chat later.

{ 274 }

"I'm sorry you aren't your typical sunny self, Amy," Homer said. "It just so happens my hero today is the comedian Steven Wright." He affected Wright's lethargic style of speech. "'Curiosity killed the cat...but for a while, I was a suspect.'"

"That's funny," I said, with a smile.

"'I had to stop driving my car for a while...the tires got dizzy.'"

That quote made my laughter bubble up and spill over.

"Way to go." Scott clapped Homer on the back. "That's the first laugh—and nearly the first smile—I've seen out of Amy all day."

"Glad I could help dispel the doldrums," Homer said.

"No doldrums," I assured him. "I'm busy—that's all. I'll have your sausage biscuit ready in a few."

As I went into the kitchen to prepare Homer's meal, I wondered if Steven Wright really *was* Homer's hero of the day or if he'd pulled the quotes out of thin air simply to make me laugh. I was convinced that Homer had a photographic memory and that's why he could remember all those quotes so easily. Of course, Mr. Wright had once theorized that everyone has a photographic memory, but not everybody had film.

I'd have given Homer an extra sausage biscuit free of charge, but that would've thrown the man off course. I didn't have the heart to do that, especially since he'd been so eager to improve my state of mind. He couldn't help the fact that I had evidence in my purse that gave all the Ostermanns and Scott—the best server I'd ever had besides Jackie—strong motives for murder.

After we'd closed the café and were cleaning up, Scott tried to engage me in conversation. He was determined to cajole me out of my bad mood.

"Guru Guy was able to make you laugh, but then you were all down again," he said. "Talk to me. Maybe I can help."

I thought of a way to speak with Scott about Gladys Pridemore. "Yesterday evening, I was looking through those cookbooks that Malcolm Pridemore brought, and I got upset."

"Because he acted like they were a gift and then made you pay for them?"

"No. The books were worth what I paid for them and then some." I turned up the chair in front of me and placed it on the table to facilitate mopping. Luis typically did this job, but he'd had to leave early to pick up one of his siblings from school. "Jackie and I found Ms. Pridemore on the day she died. I can't help but think that she'd still be alive if we'd arrived earlier."

Scott came around the table and put his arm around me. "You can't beat yourself up about that. There's no way you could've saved that woman."

"How do you know?"

"A few minutes either way couldn't have made that much of a difference...right?" he asked. "And, either way, you can't change it."

"Working with the Ostermanns, you must've known Ms. Pridemore. I'd never set eyes on her until that day. What was she like?"

Scott moved away from me and resumed putting chairs atop tables. "I never met her either."

I went back to helping stack the chairs, but I wasn't ready to let the subject go. He'd asked me to talk. Someone should've warned Scott to be careful what he wished for. "What about the Ostermanns? How did they feel about her?"

"I guess they liked her okay." He kept his eyes downcast.

"Was she a good landlord?"

"I don't know," he said.

"I'm sorry." I moved to another table. "Here you are trying to cheer me up, and I've brought you down."

"No, you haven't. I just..." He shrugged one shoulder. "I didn't know Ms. Pridemore."

"So, tell me about HJ," I said."How in the world did he break an animatronic spider?"

Scott met my eyes and grinned. "The idiot tripped and fell on it."

"I can understand that." I continued putting chairs on tables. "Unless it's a super clear night, it's really dark in that maze...and then there are the fog machines. It's a wonder more people don't trip."

"Oh, no. We make sure there's nothing in the guests' way. HJ was drunk when he fell and broke the spider."

"Really? Oh, wow." I laughed. "No wonder he didn't want his dad to find out."

"Harry would've been enraged. He hates that HJ drinks too much." Scott put the last chair up and surveyed the dining room to make sure we got them all. "I'll get the mop."

Jackie and I were the last to leave. I could tell she'd been dawdling in order to speak with me.

"Have you made a decision about the partnership?" I asked as I put the deposit into the bank envelope.

"No, I'm still thinking about that. But I overheard your conversation with Scott." She put her hand on my arm. "Have you really been that distressed about Gladys Pridemore's death?"

I retrieved my purse from beneath the counter. "These were in one of Ms. Pridemore's cookbooks." I spread the photographs out for Jackie to see.

"So, you were trying to find out what Scott knows," she said.

"Yes." I tapped the picture of Scott and Nadine. "Don't you agree this makes him more suspicious?"

"I don't know." She picked up the photo to examine it more closely. "I think it makes Nadine look bad." She held the photograph closer to me. "Scott doesn't appear to be enjoying this kiss. Look at where his hands are—they're on Nadine's shoulders as if he's trying to push her away."

"I didn't notice that." I sighed. "Still, if Gladys Pridemore was threatening to show this photo to Harry Ostermann, it gives both Nadine and Scott motive to kill her. Mr. Ostermann's high school football team didn't call him *Big Harry* ironically."

"Good point," Jackie said. "You like Scott, don't you?"

"I *did.* He's a great worker, and I thought that if Shelly needed to go part-time to be with her mom more, Scott would be a valuable addition to the Down South Café team."

"Yeah." She smiled slightly. "The customers love him...the old ones and the younger ones too."

I recalled Ryan's warning and said, "They'd have loved Ted Bundy too."

Chapter Eighteen

I was on my way to the police station when I noticed a car on the right side of the road. As I neared the vehicle, a woman got out and flagged me down. I recognized the woman as Nadine Ostermann, so I swung over to the shoulder behind her car.

She approached my car before I could get out, and I put down my window. "Nadine, what's wrong?"

"Aw, I don't know. The thing just stopped on me."

"Is Harry on his way?" I asked.

"No...um...I can't get him or HJ to answer their phones. Would you mind giving me a lift home?"

Actually, yes, I do mind...but I can't tell Nadine that. "Not at all. I hope you don't care if we make a

Gayle Leeson

detour first. I have to drop some food off at the police station."

"Really? I didn't think the Down South Café offered delivery services." Nadine went around to the passenger side of my car.

"Just a second," I said, getting out and moving the box of food into the back seat. "There you go." I gave Nadine a tight smile. "We all make exceptions for boyfriends...don't we?"

She laughed. "We sure do. I remember those good old days of being young and in love."

"What're you saying?" I kept my tone light, but I was serious. "You aren't in love anymore?"

"Oh, sure...but things change as you get older." Her smile faded. "I miss my youth. Enjoy it while you have it."

I checked my rearview mirror to make sure nothing was coming before I pulled back onto the road. "Oh, now, you aren't *that* old, Nadine."

"Maybe not...but I'm not that young either." She adjusted the vent in front of her so the cool air would blow directly into her face. "I'm glad you came along when you did. Harry and HJ wouldn't have missed me until suppertime."

"Should we call and have your car towed?" I asked.

"No. I'm positive Harry can fix it." She turned to look at my profile. "How do you like working with Scott?"

"He's one of the best servers I've ever had. I don't know how we'd have managed without him while Shelly has been away." I explained about Shelly's mom.

"I'm sorry to hear that," Nadine said. "But you're absolutely right about Scott being a wonderful employee. Anything he sets his mind to, he really gives it his all."

My mind flashed to the photograph of her and Scott, and I successfully managed not to cringe. *Should I change the subject or keep her talking about Scott to see if I can determine how she feels about him? Is it love or merely an affair? Maybe I can even get a confession! So...yeah...keep her talking about Scott.*

"Jackie was saying earlier today that all our customers like Scott," I said.

"Oh, ours do too." She gave a wistful smile I'd have missed had I not glanced over at her in that instant. "But, then, why wouldn't they? He's something else."

I didn't answer. What could I have possibly said to that? This time, I *did* change the subject. "It's good that you and Harry have HJ there with you. I mean, I know it's probably sad for all of you that he's going through a divorce, but it's—"

"It doesn't bother me." Nadine's voice took on a bitter edge. "I never did like HJ's wife. She was spoiled and demanding...wanted everything handed to her on a silver platter. She might've had HJ fooled, and Harry too, for a while, but I had her figured out from the very beginning."

"Did they have any children?"

"No. I believe both Harry and HJ were both sad about that initially. Harry would've loved to have had a grandbaby running around." She flicked her wrist. "I said better no child than a child with a woman who'd constantly badmouth you to your own flesh and blood. Besides, HJ is only thirty...and he still has some growing up to do before he even thinks about having a family."

By then we'd reached the police station. I parked and turned to Nadine. "I won't be but a minute. Shall I leave the engine running?"

"Oh, no. I'll go in with you," she said. "I need to ask the sheriff not to tow my car before Harry can get it running again."

Nadine insisted on carrying the box of food, saying it was the least she could do since I was being so helpful and all. I clutched my purse to my side, afraid Nadine would somehow figure out that delivering food wasn't my only purpose in going to the station.

Both Ryan and Sheriff Billings looked startled to see Nadine accompanying me into the office, but they recovered quickly.

"I don't know what's in here," Nadine told them, "but it sure does smell good."

"I can't disagree with you on that." Sheriff Billings took the box from Nadine. "Let me give you a hand with that."

"Ryan, could I speak with you privately for a moment?" I asked.

"Of course." He led me down the hallway to the locker room. The lockers were painted blue, and there was a wooden bench against the wall across from them.

"Which one is yours?" I asked.

"Number seven." He gently took my shoulders and turned me to face him. "What's she doing here?"

"Her car broke down, and I'm giving her a lift home."

"What's wrong with her car?"

"I have no idea. Maybe her tires got dizzy." I giggled.

He frowned. "What?"

"It's a joke...I'll...never mind."

"Why didn't she call her husband?" Ryan asked. "Did she call and ask you to take her home?"

"No. I saw her car on the side of the road. She said she tried phoning her husband and her son, but neither answered." I took the pictures from my purse. "These fell out of one of the cookbooks I bought from Malcolm Pridemore. They aren't the best photographs I've ever seen, but they prove that all the Ostermanns—and Scott—might've had a motive for getting rid of Ms. Pridemore."

Ryan tucked the photos inside his shirt. "We'd better go back out there now, but let's make our reason for needing privacy look legitimate."

He kissed me then...a long, passionate kiss that I didn't want to end.

When we walked back into the office a respectable distance apart, Sheriff Billings said to Ryan, "I hate to say this, son, but that shade of lipstick is not your color."

I felt my face flush. Ryan was grinning, but his cheeks pinkened as well.

"I am glad your private conversation ended well, though." Sheriff Billings winked at Nadine. "I don't know who'd get custody of me if these two were to ever split up."

"We'd arrange for joint custody," I said. "Otherwise, you'd starve to death when Molly had to leave town."

"But the sheriff doesn't need to worry about that." Ryan gave me a warm smile, and I could feel my blush deepen.

"All right, we've teased Amy enough," Sheriff Billings said. "Let's eat."

"It's obvious how much they care about you," Nadine said, as we drove toward her house.

"I care about them too," I said, wondering where Nadine was going with this conversation. With someone else, I might've thought it was an innocent observation. But Nadine put me on my guard.

"I'm glad it was Sheriff Billings who answered the 9-1-1 call when you and Jackie found Ms. Pridemore. Another officer might've found it suspicious...the two of you just happening to find that poor old lady clinging to life like that."

I tried to keep the anger that sparked inside me from becoming evident when I spoke. "I'm sure *any* investigating officer would've understood right away that Jackie and I had nothing to do with Ms. Pridemore's condition. If we had, why would we have been trying so hard to save her?"

"Now, there's no need to get all defensive with me," Nadine said, with a hoot of laughter. "I was merely saying I wouldn't have wanted to be in your situation."

I so wanted to put her out on the side of the road. "Trust me, neither of us relished being in that situation either. It was terrible. I only wish we'd have gotten there in time to help her."

"There was nothing you could do...nothing anybody could do. I'm surprised she lasted as long as she did, you know, from what the doctors said."

"What was Ms. Pridemore like?" I asked.

"She was your typical little old woman, I reckon. Ornery, nosy, cheap..."

"It doesn't sound like there was much love lost between you." I flipped on my signal light and got ready to turn onto the Pridemore property.

"I guess not," Nadine said. "I mean, I'm sorry that she died and all, but even in the end, she tried to stick it to us with this lease-to-own business."

"Really?" I drove up the driveway to the mobile home as far as I could. Harry and HJ's vehicles prevented me from advancing any further. So...if they were home, why hadn't they answered their phones?

"...Malcolm Pridemore as the administrator of her estate," Nadine was saying. "And if he can find any loophole whatsoever, he'll kick us off this land, and we'll lose every cent we put into it. Wait and see, it'll happen. Between you and me, I wish we'd never set eyes on this place." She opened the door. "Thanks again for the ride, Amy. I appreciate your help."

"Anytime," I said.

Ryan called as I was on my way home. "Are you alone?" he asked.

"Yes, I dropped Nadine off just a couple of minutes ago. Funny thing, both Harry and HJ appeared to be home, so I don't know why Nadine couldn't reach them."

Sheriff Billings spoke then. "Amy, you're on speaker. Nadine probably didn't even try to reach her husband or her son, and I don't think there's anything wrong with her car. I think she wanted to get you alone to find out what you know about Gladys Pridemore's death and maybe about the estate situation."

"She did say that Jackie and I were lucky that you were the investigating officer when we found Ms. Pridemore...and that really ticked me off." I braked for a squirrel racing across the road. "I told Nadine that any law enforcement officer who worked that crime scene would have been able to see that Jackie and I had nothing to do with Ms. Pridemore's death. If we had, we wouldn't have been trying to save the woman."

"What was her reaction to that?" Ryan asked.

"She said that given what the doctors said, she was surprised Ms. Pridemore was able to hang on for as long as she did."

"You said nothing about the way Gladys Pridemore was murdered, did you?" I could hear the apprehension in Sheriff Billings' voice.

"Of course not. I didn't even let on that I knew Ms. Pridemore had been murdered."

"Good job." He let out a breath.

"How about the photos?" Ryan asked. "Did you mention them to anyone other than Sheriff Billings and me?"

"Only Jackie. I was especially disappointed about the one with Scott and Nadine. I'd hoped Scott was as nice as he seemed and would continue to fill in for Shelly." I sighed. "Jackie pointed out that Scott appears to be pushing Nadine away in the photograph, but I'm still concerned about trusting him. I'm thinking of calling and telling him not to come in tomorrow."

"Don't do that," Sheriff Billings said quickly. "I'd prefer you act as if you don't suspect Scott...or anyone else. Behave as you normally would."

"But that's hard," I said. "Even today, Scott was aware that I was acting differently. I told him it was because the cookbooks Mr. Pridemore brought to the café made me wonder again if Jackie and I could've saved Ms. Pridemore had we arrived at the house sooner."

"What did he say to that?" the sheriff asked.

"His response was pretty much the same as Nadine's—that we couldn't have made a difference no matter what."

"Sheriff, when you and I were discussing this earlier, you indicated Amy should avoid Scott and the Ostermanns," Ryan said. "Now you want her to keep employing Scott at the café?"

"I do. Unless Shelly comes back or the part-time waitress can cover her shifts, it would look curious for Amy to let Scott go."

"I agree with Sheriff Billings," I said. "Besides, we need the help."

Ryan huffed. "Just don't get caught alone with him."

"Or with any of the Ostermanns," Sheriff Billings added. "And be leery of Malcolm Pridemore too."

"Why Mr. Pridemore?" I asked. "There weren't any compromising photographs of him."

"He might've taken those out of the book," Ryan said.

"What? You think the photos in the cookbook could have been a setup?" On the one hand, I was shocked. But on the other hand, I wondered why I hadn't thought of it before. I'd assumed I'd lost my naivete back when I'd worked for Lou Lou Holman. Obviously not. "But Mr. Pridemore wasn't living on the property, and Nadine Ostermann told me he rarely visited. Don't you think the odds are slim that Gladys Pridemore had any dirt on her brother-in-law?"

"The dirt doesn't need to be recent to be effective," Sheriff Billings said. "We simply want you to exercise the utmost caution."

Chapter Nineteen

Thursday morning was off to a good start. Traffic among the diners was steady, but we weren't so busy we couldn't chat with our favorite patrons. Dilly and Walter had come into the café in high spirits and were wondering where to go on their next day trip. Despite several good suggestions, they didn't settle on a destination. However, Jackie and I both decided we needed to take a day trip soon ourselves. Homer's hero was some obscure German poet, and Luis and Scott had good-naturedly argued all morning about which teams were going to make it to the World Series this year.

At around eleven-thirty, Jackie was serving a group of travelers who were on their way to visit Monticello, the historic home of Thomas Jefferson.

"Monticello," she said, upon delivering the group's orders to the kitchen. "That's somewhere we didn't think of to tell Dilly and Walter. Wonder if they've ever been?"

"I don't know. I haven't," I said. "Have you?"

"No. We should check it out sometime." She noticed my eyes widen, and she turned to see what I was looking at through the window between the kitchen and the dining room. She groaned softly when she saw Harry, Nadine, and HJ Ostermann coming through the door.

We both gasped when we saw that Malcolm Pridemore was with them.

"What's up with that?" I asked quietly.

"No idea. Maybe they're going to sell the property to Mr. Pridemore after all." She saw that Scott was seating them and said, "Good. I'll let him deal with them."

Still, I had a hard time letting it go. When Scott came to the window with the orders, I motioned for him to come inside the kitchen.

"That's weird," I said.

"What is?"

"The Ostermanns having brunch with Malcolm Pridemore." I peeped out the window at the animated group. "I thought they didn't like each other."

"Beats me. But they all seem to be getting along." He smiled. "And that's good...right?"

"That's great." Either Scott was a master of deception, or he was even more naïve that I was.

Scott went back out to wait on his customers, and I resumed cooking. It wasn't but a few minutes after my conversation with Scott that Jackie came into the kitchen.

"Hi. Ryan is here to see you. I'll take over the grill."

"Okay. Thanks." I took off my plastic gloves. "I'll be back as quickly as I can."

"Take your time."

I went out into the dining room. Ryan was standing by the door, and the two of us went outside. He put his arm around me and walked me to the edge of the parking lot where we wouldn't easily be observed by the diners.

"What's going on?" I asked. "Is everything all right?"

"Yeah. I just wanted to let you know that we had an expert enlarge and examine the picture of the weedy lot that was in the cookbook. We're fairly certain it shows a large marijuana crop."

I gaped. "Are you kidding? Maybe they have one of those medical marijuana licenses or something."

"We checked with the DEA, and they don't. We're sending drones over there to take aerial photos of the fields, and then we'll take action based on what we find."

I hugged him. "Be careful."

"Hmm...this is nice, but you know, I might be putting my life on the line..." He tried to suppress a grin but couldn't.

I gave him a kiss that was on par with the one he'd given me at the police station the day before. "Better?"

"Best. I might have to take the rest of the day off to recover."

I laughed. "Seriously, be careful, all right?"

"I will. I'd like for you to exercise some caution today too. I don't know what our actions might set into motion."

"Uh...yeah. That's why I'm concerned about *you*."

He dropped a light kiss on my lips. "I'll be fine."

When I walked back into the café alone, I felt as if every person in the place was staring a hole through me. My cheeks burned as I walked through the dining room and wished I'd taken the back door into the kitchen.

"Well, *that* must've been interesting," Jackie said when she glanced up at me. "Your face is redder than mine, and I'm standing in front of a hot grill."

"Please swap back with me. I don't want to have to go out there in front of those people again with all of them gawking at me."

She chuckled. "All right. But you owe me."

"Cancel the Ostermanns' and Pridemore's orders please," Scott said from the window. "Pridemore got a call, said a matter of utmost importance had arisen, and left."

"But their meals are done," Jackie said. "See if you can get the Ostermanns, at least, to stay."

"No can do, Jackie. They're already gone." He lifted his palms. "How about Luis and I eat their food, and I'll pay for it?"

"You don't have to pay," I said. "I just don't want good food to go to waste."

I slipped on gloves, and Jackie handed me the spatula.

"A matter of utmost importance calls me to the dining room," she said.

I rolled my eyes.

Scott laughed. "Good one, Jack-rocks."

"One time," she told him, putting her index finger in front of his face. "You get a one-time pass. Call me that again and see what happens."

He winked at me before following her into the dining room.

Their actions seemed so relaxed that I smiled. I desperately wanted things to be normal around here, but I knew that just wishing wouldn't make it so.

I was cleaning the grill after the café closed for the day when I heard Scott and another man arguing. I knew it wasn't Luis because he'd just gone out back to take the trash to the Dumpster. I stepped over to the door between the kitchen and the dining room and opened it slightly.

HJ was pleading with Scott. "Come on, man, I need your help."

"Sorry, dude. I can't this evening. I promised my sister I'd come over to her house."

"This is urgent," HJ said.

"I can't do it."

HJ raised his hands to Scott's chest and shoved him backward. Scott stumbled, but he didn't fall.

"Don't bother coming back to work at the corn maze either." HJ stormed out of the café.

I hurried out of the kitchen to check on Scott. "Are you all right?"

"Yeah. HJ is being a jerk. No big deal."

"What's his problem?" I asked.

"He wanted me to work tonight, but I've already made plans with my sister."

Jackie came in from the patio where she'd been cleaning the tables and chairs. "What's up with HJ Ostermann? He just scratched off and threw gravels all over the parking lot. I hope everyone's car is all right."

Scott gave us a lopsided smile. "A few pockmarks might improve the looks of my ride."

"HJ wanted Scott to work tonight," I told Jackie, although I remembered that HJ's parting words were *don't bother coming back to work at the corn maze either.* I turned back to Scott. "What kind of work did he want you to do?"

"Farming."

"Farming? Tonight?" I was confused. "Who farms at night?"

"People who have something to hide," Scott said. "That's why I made up the excuse about my sister. I don't want to be involved in HJ's shady business."

"Well, that...that's good thinking," I said. I hadn't told anyone—not even Jackie—what Ryan had shared with me. But I took the fact that Scott had made up an excuse in order to avoid helping HJ as a good sign. He wasn't involved in HJ's illegal business, and he could still work for the Down South Café. I patted his arm. "I'm sure you're making the right choice."

"Me, too." Jackie patted Scott's other arm. "Apparently, we're your moms now. Make good choices, kid."

"I'm as old as you guys are," he said.

"Doesn't matter. Amy mothers everybody, including Homer. I'm going out to finish work on that patio furniture."

"I'll mop the dining room," Scott said.

Luis came through from the kitchen. "Jackie, I'll help you with the patio."

"Don't you need to pick up your sister from school?" she asked.

"She'll be fine waiting a few extra minutes."

"Go get her." Jackie acted as if she were shooing him out the door. "The furniture isn't *that* dirty."

I went back to the kitchen and resumed work on the grill. I'd been listening to an interesting audiobook, so I put in Bluetooth earbuds and listened to the book as I worked. Half an hour later, I'd cleaned the grill and wiped down the other appliances.

I turned off the audiobook and dropped the earbuds in my apron pocket. It was awfully quiet out there. Had everyone gone already?

"Hello!" I called, as I stepped out of the kitchen.

Jackie's purse still sat next to mine behind the counter. I immediately went to the patio to help her finish cleaning the furniture. She wasn't there, but two of the chairs were overturned.

Could she be in the bathroom?

I stepped back into the dining room. "Jackie!" No answer. I hurried to the bathroom door and knocked. "Jackie, are you in there?"

Nothing.

I took my phone from my apron pocket so I could call Ryan. I'd received a text from a caller whose number had been blocked. It said:

Have your boyfriend call off the investigation of the Pridemore property if you ever want to see your cousin in one piece again.

Well, way to go hiding your number, HJ, I thought. *I'd have never guessed it was you.*

I called Ryan.

"Hey, sweetheart," he answered.

"We've got a problem," I said. "HJ Ostermann has Jackie."

"I don't think so. I'm sitting here looking at HJ Ostermann. He's talking with Sheriff Billings."

"He's *what*? Then he's done something with her...he's...How long has he been there?"

"About twenty minutes. Calm down and tell me what's going on."

I took a shaky breath and told Ryan about the text.

"Stay where you are," he said. "I'll head over to the Pridemore house."

"All right." My hands were trembling as I ended the call. I hoped Ryan realized that I meant *all right* about him heading over to the Pridemore house, not *all right* about me staying where I was. No way would Jackie stay here at the café if she thought my life was in danger. And there was no way I wasn't going after her.

As I drove, I mulled everything over in my head. Scott was gone. Jackie was gone. Had everything Scott said to us been a lie? Was he involved in the marijuana operation on the Pridemore property? Was he trying to help HJ "farm" before the Winter Garden Police Department raided the place? Why was HJ talking with Sheriff Billings?

Nothing made sense to me. All I knew was that I had to get to Jackie as quickly as I could.

I drove to the Pridemore property and headed straight to the Ostermann's mobile home. I got out, killed the engine, and pounded on the door.

"Hello! It's Amy Flowers!"

I pounded on the door again. When I still didn't get a response, I tried to open the door. It was locked.

I ran around to the other side and rained my fists on the back door, but again, there was no response. I peeped through the window, cupping my hands around my face, to see if maybe Jackie was inside tied to a chair or something, but all I could see was the clutter that filled nearly every square inch of Nadine Ostermann's kitchen.

"Jackie!" I yelled. I was quiet as I pressed my ear against the window, but I couldn't hear anything over the beating of my own heart.

I turned and looked out over the fields. From my vantage point, I could see much of the property. Maybe they were in the marijuana fields, but I didn't even know where that was. I needed Gladys Pridemore's binoculars...and they were in Nadine's kitchen.

A charge at the door with my left shoulder showed me right away that I was not superhero material. Other than causing me pain in my shoulder and nearly making me fall back onto the grass, that feat accomplished nothing.

I closed my eyes, listened, and thought. Where would Scott take Jackie?

The corn maze!

I ran through the fields. I approached the maze from the side, but I remembered Scott telling me that he went in and out of the maze through the corn stalks. He didn't need to navigate the maze every time.

Fighting my way over stalks of corn that were taller than my head was harder than I'd anticipated. I started to call out to Jackie, but I was suddenly afraid. What if my calling to her made him hit her to keep her from answering?

I made it through one row of corn and was inside the maze. Still, I didn't know where I was with regard to the rest of the maze or the surrounding area. I stood and tried to get my bearings. In the distance, I heard a siren. Help was on the way. I felt my pockets for my phone and realized I'd left it in the car.

I scrambled through another row of corn. Still, I couldn't see anything except cornstalks and hay. But this time, I heard a muffled cry.

Jackie.

Still afraid she wasn't alone and that I'd cause some harm to come to her, I remained silent and tried to concentrate on the location of that scream. I carefully made my way to the left and saw a dead end where there was a creature covered with a tarp. Before I could turn and go in the opposite direction, the creature moved. It was still likely an animatronic character, but I wasn't going to leave any stone—or tarp—unturned.

I walked over and ripped off the tarp. "Jackie!"

Her hands and feet were bound and there was duct tape over her mouth, and she was furious.

"Sorry," I said. "This'll probably hurt." I quickly ripped the tape off. "Where's Scott?"

"Scott? No, it's—"

Before she could finish her sentence, she headbutted me and knocked me to the ground. Almost immediately, I realized she'd done that to keep Harry Ostermann from hitting me on the back of the head. When Jackie crashed into me, I fell into Harry and caused him to stumble. Before he could right himself, I grabbed him by the ankle and pulled. He started falling like a giant oak, and I rolled to the side to keep from getting smushed.

Of course, Harry rolled onto his side and seized me before I could get out of his reach. He hauled me back toward him and drew back a meaty fist.

I raised my knees to my chest and kicked as hard as I could. Harry let out a raspy breath, and I managed to clamber out from under him. He was now lying face down on the ground in front of me. I dove onto his back.

Unfortunately, I underestimated Big Harry Ostermann. He was able to pull himself into a standing position with me clinging to his back. As he stood, I had to wrap my arms around his neck, afraid I'd fall. And, then, he tried to shake me off. I held on for dear life, but I wasn't sure how long I could keep it up.

"Ryan, where are you?" I yelled as loudly as I could.

"Right behind you."

A quick look to my right ensured that I wasn't hallucinating. There was my gorgeous boyfriend standing beside me in his uniform with his gun drawn. It was the sexiest sight I'd ever seen.

"I love you," I said.

"Ostermann, I have a Glock 22 pointed at the back of your head loaded with fifteen rounds," Ryan said. "I want you to slowly raise your hands and, after Amy drops off your back, get on your knees."

I let go and slid onto the ground. I stepped to the side and allowed Ryan to handcuff Harry. Then I went to help Jackie with her restraints.

"Is this where the credits roll, and you and Ryan ride into the sunset on a horse with no name?" she asked wryly.

"Don't be ridiculous. The horse is named Butterbean."

Chapter Twenty

The paramedics had insisted on taking Jackie to the emergency room to get her checked out. I rode with her and asked her how Harry had gotten the drop on her.

"I was on the patio cleaning tables, singing along to the radio, and I saw Harry pull up. I didn't think much about it. I figured he was either looking for HJ or Scott."

"Was Scott still there then?" I asked.

"No, he'd left about five minutes earlier. Harry saw me and came around the side of the café. I went over to tell him that we were closed and that Scott and HJ weren't there, and he grabbed me and pulled me outside."

I rubbed my hand over my face. "I'm so sorry I didn't hear you. I'll never listen to anything while I clean ever again."

"Nonsense. We'll just know to never leave the doors unlocked before and after business hours again." She took my hand. "Thanks for coming after me."

"You'd have done the same for me."

"True." She grinned. "But I'm tougher than you are."

"Uh-huh. Who was it again who got the best of Big Hairy Ostrich-Man?"

"Ryan," she said.

I couldn't argue with that.

When we got to the hospital, I remained with Jackie while the doctor was examining her. She had some cuts and bruises, but she didn't have a concussion.

The doctor was a woman not much older than Jackie and me, and she had a soothing voice. "You've suffered physical and emotional trauma, Ms. Fonseca. I'll be happy to refer you to a therapist if you need to talk with someone."

"I'm fine," Jackie said.

"I know." The doctor handed Jackie a card. "This is a hotline you can call any time of the day or night."

"Don't be too proud or too stubborn to accept it,"
I told Jackie.

She took the card reluctantly. "I'm not a therapy
kind of person."

The doctor smiled gently. "Every feeling you
might go through for the next few days—from ex-
haustion to denial to anger to confusion—is normal.
Understand that, be kind to yourself, and talk with
someone if need be."

When the doctor left the room, a nurse came in.
"There's a whole bunch of people here to see you.
One young man, in particular, is pretty anxious
about it. I think everyone else can wait until you're
released. It won't be much longer."

"I'll step outside and tell Roger he can see you
now," I said.

Before I could even get all the way into the hallway, Roger hugged me. "How is she, Flowerpot?"

"She's fine." I pulled him to the side of the door
before the nurse came out and knocked us both sideways. "Whatever you do, don't baby her. You'll just
tick her off."

"I know, I know. But I thought I'd stop for rocky
road on the way home."

I smiled. "Let Mom and Aunt Bess bring the ice
cream. She needs to stay at the Big House tonight."

"She all right with that?" he asked.

"Probably not, but Aunt Bess will make her."

That evening I was sitting on the porch when Ryan's red convertible drove into my driveway. My lips curved into a smile...but straightened right back out when I saw another car park behind him.

Who is that? Oh, no...it's his parents.

I stood. "Hi."

"Hi." Ryan climbed the steps and gave me a quick peck on the lips. "How are you feeling?"

"I'm all right," I said. "A little sore."

"I imagine you'll be even achier tomorrow." Michelle examined my face. "It could've been worse. It's no way near as bad as the time I got mugged in Nevada. David was at a conference and hadn't called to let me know he'd be late."

"She always has to add that part," David said, with a glum half-smile.

"It explains why I was standing on the street alone when that...that *villain*...came out of nowhere." After her admonishing glance at her husband, Michelle turned her attention back to me. "He tried to take my purse, but I fought him tooth and nail and held him off until the police got there. I still have a scar on my hand that I got during the struggle." She thrust out her left hand.

I couldn't see the first sign of a scar, but I frowned at her hand as if I did. "Wow."

She nodded. "I know. I was lucky not to have suffered worse injuries."

David grinned. "Ryan said you'd leaped on that man's back and was giving him what-for when he got there."

"I had to do something. He was holding my cousin hostage."

"Well, I say good for you," David said. "If you ever think you're going down, at least, go down fighting."

"Amy is fortunate that Ryan was there to save her," Michelle said. "I'd prefer everyone to avoid fights when possible...especially Ryan...but nobody listens to me. David, go get that afghan for Amy from the car please."

He immediately did as she asked. So, obviously, *he* listened to this woman who preferred everyone to avoid fights and who'd been in at least three that I knew about.

David returned carrying a peacock blue and white granny-square afghan.

"Oh, my goodness," I breathed. "That's gorgeous."

"Ryan told us about your fancy room," Michelle said. "I hope this afghan matches. He seems to think it will."

"It's perfect." I hugged the afghan to my chest.

"Good. It might help you rest better." Michelle looked away. "I had a hard time sleeping after my ordeal."

"I can imagine." I ran my hand over the afghan. "This is so soft. Poor Hilda Dinsmore can't compete with this caliber of work."

Michelle beamed. "Well...no...she really can't, can she?"

And we said it together: "Bless her heart."

"We need to go and let Amy get some rest," David said. "Do take some aspirin or something before you go to bed. You'll be sorer than you think you'll be tomorrow morning."

"Ryan, take care of her." Michelle waved as they strolled to their car.

"I can't believe your mom gave this to me." I looked at the afghan. "It's beautiful."

"You're beautiful. And I did pay her for the afghan, but that's beside the point."

I laughed. "Did I tell you how happy I was to see you today?"

"Did I tell you how unsurprised I was to see you?" He draped an arm over my shoulders and led me into the house. "When Scott went by the café and saw that your car was gone, he called Ivy immediately."

I frowned. "Why would he call Ivy? How does Scott even *know* Ivy?"

"She's his sister." Ryan laughed at my shocked expression.

"Huh...they *are* like Daphne and Shaggy from *Scooby Doo*." I shook my head. "But why didn't he tell us they're brother and sister?"

"Well, when Ms. Pridemore was killed while Scott was working for the Ostermanns, Ivy instructed him not to let on to anyone that they were related. She was afraid it would compromise the investigation."

"But why did he continue working there?" I asked.

"To see what he could learn. For the record, he didn't know about the marijuana patch until today when HJ asked him to help get rid of it."

We sat on the sofa, and I placed my legs across Ryan's lap. He covered them up with his mom's afghan.

"They were *all* in on it then?"

Ryan shook his head. "Only Harry and Nadine. HJ found out about it and tried to eradicate the crop before the DEA came in and seized it...which is what happened after the paramedics took you and Jackie out of there. He didn't want his parents to get arrested. That's why he came to see Sheriff Billings. He was trying to figure a way out for them."

I rested my head against the sofa cushion. "And did the Ostermanns confess to killing Gladys Pridemore too?"

"Nadine did." Ryan slipped my sandals from my feet and began to massage my arches. "Does that hurt?"

I shook my head. "It feels wonderful."

"Good." He continued his narrative. "Nadine thought she'd get a lighter sentence if she blamed everything on Harry, so she did."

"Will she get a lighter sentence?"

"I don't think so," he said. "She was every bit as involved as her husband."

"She's the one who called the café that Saturday, wasn't she?"

"Yep. Nadine wanted to make sure Ms. Pridemore was found and declared dead so the will would be executed. With the woman being pretty much a recluse, having food delivered to her seemed like the best option."

I scoffed. "Naturally. I mean, they couldn't find her themselves. That would look bad."

"Let's not talk about the Ostermanns anymore. Let's talk about you...and me."

My eyes lowered to my hands. He was going to ask me about what I said. I *could* say I'd told him I loved him in the heat of the moment...but I didn't want to lie. I loved Ryan Hall. I wasn't exactly sure when I fell in love with this man, but I was absolutely head over heels. And I wasn't afraid to admit it. I raised my eyes to his.

"I love you too," he said.

Recipes from the Down South Café

Low Carb White Fish Pomodoro

This recipe is courtesy of Sommer of A Spicy Perspective. *Get more information (including nutrition and Sommer's tips) at*
https://www.aspicyperspective.com/low-carb-white-fish-pomodoro/

Ingredients
3-4 skinless white fish fillets (grouper, cod, monkfish, halibut)

1 tablespoon olive oil

3 cloves garlic, minced

1 shallot, peeled and finely chopped

28 ounces crushed tomatoes (1 can)

1/2 cup roughly chopped basil

1 teaspoon honey

Salt and pepper

Instructions

Place a large skillet over medium heat. Add the oil. Salt and pepper the fish fillets on both sides. Once the oil is hot, sear the fish fillets until cooked through. For thin fillets like grouper, cook 2 minutes per side. For thicker fillets like cod, cook 4 minutes per side. Remove from the skillet and set aside.

Add the garlic and shallots to the skillet. Saute for 2-3 minutes to soften. Then add in the crushed tomatoes and honey. Stir and simmer for 5 minutes. Taste, and salt and pepper as needed.

Stir in the fresh basil and add the fish fillets back to the skillet. Simmer another 1-2 minutes to reheat the fish. Serve warm as-is or with a side of raw zucchini noodles.

Diet Cola Brownies

You can find recipes for these all over the Internet. I tried them and loved them. I didn't tell my son they were made with Diet Coke and Low-Fat Brownie mix, and he loved them too!

Ingredients
12 oz can Diet Cola
1 box of brownie mix (I used Betty Crocker Low-Fat Fudge Brownie Mix.)

Instructions

Empty brownie mix into large bowl. Add 12 oz. diet cola. Using a handheld mixer or whisk, combine until batter is free of lumps.

Pour mixture into a 9 x 9 pan treated with nonstick cooking spray.

Bake according to brownie mix instructions, adding an additional 5 to 10 minutes baking time.

Links to Additional Foods Prepared in *Apples and Alibis*

Stuffed Pepper Casserole –

https://www.bettycrocker.com/recipes/stuffed-pepper-casserole/55349f80-93ac-4bdc-bdca-2ebbe4c59424

Crock Pot Party Mix –

https://www.gimmesomeoven.com/slow-cooker-chex-mix-recipe/

Homemade Belgian Waffles -

https://thesaltymarshmallow.com/homemade-belgian-waffle-recipe/

Also by Gayle Leeson

Down South Café Mystery Series
The Calamity Café
Silence of the Jams
Honey-Baked Homicide

Ghostly Fashionista Mystery Series
Designs On Murder
Perils and Lace

Kinsey Falls Chick-Lit Series
Hightail It to Kinsey Falls
Putting Down Roots in Kinsey Falls
Sleighing It In Kinsey Falls

Victoria Square Series (With Lorraine Bartlett)
Yule Be Dead
Murder Ink

Embroidery Mystery Series (Written as Amanda Lee)

The Quick and The Thread

Stitch Me Deadly

Thread Reckoning

The Long Stitch Goodnight

Thread on Arrival

Cross-Stitch Before Dying

Thread End

Wicked Stitch

The Stitching Hour

Better Off Thread

Cake Decorating Mystery Series (Written as Gayle Trent)

Murder Takes the Cake

Dead Pan

Killer Sweet Tooth

Battered to Death

Killer Wedding Cake

Myrtle Crumb Mystery Series (Written as Gayle Trent)

The Party Line (short story/prequel)

Between A Clutch and a Hard Place

When Good Bras Go Bad

Claus of Death

Soup...Er...Myrtle!

Perp and Circumstance

ABOUT THE AUTHOR

Gayle Leeson is known for her cozy mysteries. She also writes as Gayle Trent and Amanda Lee. To eliminate confusion going forward, Gayle is writing under the name Gayle Leeson only. She and her family live in Southwest Virginia with Cooper, the Great Pyrenees in the photograph with Gayle, and a small pride of lions (cats, really, but humor them).

Gayle Leeson

Gayle invites you to sign up for her newsletter and receive excerpts of some of her books:

https://forms.aweber.com/form/14/1780369214.htm

Social Media Links:
Twitter:

@GayleTrent

Facebook:

https://www.facebook.com/GayleLeeson/

BookBub:

https://www.bookbub.com/profile/gayle-leeson

Goodreads:

https://www.goodreads.com/author/show/426208.Gayle_Trent

CPSIA information can be obtained
at www.ICGtesting.com
Printed in the USA
FSHW011328271219
65518FS